Len K. Abbott

LOVE IS THE CROOKED THING
STORIES BY LEE K. ABBOTT

Columbus

ALGONQUIN BOOKS OF CHAPEL HILL   1986

Aug. 22, 1990

Algonquin Books of Chapel Hill
Post Office Box 2225, Chapel Hill, North Carolina 27515-2225
© 1982, 1983, 1984, 1985, 1986 Lee K. Abbott. All rights reserved.
Printed in the United States of America

The author is indebted to the National Endowment for the Arts and to the Ohio Arts
Council for fellowships that aided him in the completion of this book.

The stories in this book, many in different form, first appeared in the following
magazines and journals: "Stand in a Row and Learn," *The Missouri Review*; "The
Purpose of This Creature Man" and "Be Free, Die Young," *The Ohio Review*; "We
Get Smashed and Our Endings Are Swift," *The South Carolina Review*; "When Our
Dream World Finds Us, and These Hard Times Are Gone," *The New Orleans
Review*; "The Eldest of Things," *Crazyhorse*; "The Final Proof of Fate and Circum-
stance," *The Georgia Review*; "The Unfinished Business of Childhood," *Carolina
Quarterly*; "Love Is the Crooked Thing," *The Agni Review*; "Martians" (under the
title "The Other World I See"), *The North American Review*; "Having the Human
Thing of Joy," *Crosscurrents: A Quarterly*.

Library of Congress Cataloging-in-Publication Data

Abbott, Lee K., 1947–
   Love is the crooked thing.
   I. Title.
PS3551.B262L6 1986 813'.54 85-26823
ISBN 0-912697-30-X

For Pammy Jo, Sweetheart of the Rodeo

CONTENTS

LOVE IS THE CROOKED THING

Porpozec ciebie nie prosze dorzanin albo zyolpocz ciwego.

John Cheever, "A Vision of the World"

WHEN OUR DREAM WORLD FINDS US, AND THESE HARD TIMES ARE GONE

for John Vincent McCue

Every time Garland told the story (which, according to CPL Zookie Limmer, was singular and strange enough to be Foe itself), he gave it a new title, his favorites being those with sweep and miracle. With the 18th ARVN in MR3, it was "A Change in Luck This Way Comes," after what Garland called its tone of comfort in a world of predicament and baleful taints. Near Tay Ninh, in April, while the Bad Guys were conducting a lethal undertaking you know now as "human waves," Garland called it "Let My Beloved Come into This Garden," on account of its endearing puzzlements. In May, it was known as "To Any End Any Road May Run," and without interruption from CBUs or any Air America spookiness, its telling took less than fifteen minutes— from woman's arrival to her lonesome departure. Onan Motley, a Utah hillbilly on loan to the TAOR for his Canary

Island cigars and La Dolce Vita sunglasses, heard it as a Love Story of Splendor, and he clearly remembered the words *vagrant* and *impossible,* and the way Garland's face took on that weird, unlived-in look, as if in the ages between event and memory he'd lost the gist of it himself. In June, before Oogie Pringle rotated out, Garland, in exchange for a Motorola TV, repeated it to a DAO officer as "Bus Stop," but the man couldn't be sure, having heard that month many tales of infliction and hostility, plus a few of what he called "flimsy human means." After a time, though, everybody knew it as Garland H. Steeples' story—"The Girl of My Dreams"—a thing he told maybe a thousand times in 1968, always telling folks how he was stuck in this little town named Deming, New Mexico, at the Greyhound station, almost halfway between LA (which he was leaving because of some personal difficulty he'd rather not go into) and Dallas (which he thought he might visit on account of a sister named Mrs. Darlene Neff and the absolutely rich idea of prairie life and that seldom-heard discouraging word). "I was going to get a job," he told Howdy Holmes, a man who looked like a Jack Nicklaus caddy. "Live me the good life," he said. "Improve some, too." He had his mind on a car, a LeSabre, a vehicle with substance and sleek, Detroit styling, something worthy of his finer habits—which were, primarily, common sense, a wolf's smug smile and the ability to put aside vulgar needs. "I see me living in a bachelor pad," he told everybody, "maybe with a waterbed. Get me some art, too."

Anyway, Garland would say, having established who's who and what's what, into this bus station walked this woman—here his eyes would get like matched moons—with hair like wet bark. "I was struck," he told Lamont Wilson. "I'd been on the road twenty hours or so, I was a little tired, had nothing to eat but two Snickers bars and a bag of Cheetos, and when I see her, she's like food, you know, a basic, a staple." It took a half-hour for them to meet formally, Garland's brain curing like ham. "I kept imagining her in my place," he said, seeing her in frilly nighties, pedal pushers, maybe a pair of Tijuana toreador pants, black and bawdy. She was Oriental, not homey with the lingo, but, waving his arms, using his fingers and patience and pointing, he learned she was eighteen—"My own age," he said once, "how's that for luck?"—and came from a place called either the Iron Triangle or the Ir Drang Valley, a place like Mars where nobody wore underpants and they hummed all the time. She was going to be a rock-and-roll star—"Got name all pick out," she said, "The Innocent, okay?"—but right now she was working for Jesus.

"Christ plenty damn big," she said, "save villains, then go show biz. Meet Elvis Presley."

They sat for a long time, the only two in the place—a place, according to Short Time Safety Moe, more like Twilight Zone than teenage heaven, a place of swirls and murks. Garland told the girl about his Daddy Royce, who was a diesel mechanic for JLS Truck Service, and his stepmomma Tracy June, who wasn't anything yet but had her eyes peeled for opportunity, and his younger sister, Roylene, who was maybe going to do ballet if she stopped growing and was now writing a term paper on the bronchial tree. "She liked me," Garland told a spade Marine named Philly Dog. "I couldn't shut up. She was smiling and saying how cool Jesus had been to me, and I was blabbing about everything on account of how I was nervous and she was so fine and I was lonely and maybe she was, too." He told her he had a thousand talents—among them posture and respect—and his favorite subjects at Monroe High School had been geometry and the kind of history in which those above are flattened by those below, but he hadn't graduated because of this aforementioned dispute with Mr. Strojan, his Health teacher. Garland said he was a Taurus, which meant he was an ace in the steadfastness department but handicapped by shortcomings in the area of temper.

"Me, too!" she said. "Blow up fast like despot."

"I got the wanderlust," Garland added, showing her on a map so well creased it looked like human skin that he'd been to Warrenton, Oregon ("Man, that place is a drag," he said, "fish city, the smell will make you cry") and Las Vegas ("Won me fifty bucks there in a IHOP slot!") and a thousand Arizona towns all alike with dust and mean faces and speed traps. In Texas, he said, he wanted to go to the place where Kennedy got killed, then visit the Alamo, walk in the footsteps of Davy Crockett and that inventive Bowie fellow.

"Oh, big damn steps," she said.

She had a laugh, he told the boys near the Perfume River, like, well, *liquid,* free and refreshing, the kind that Little Red Riding Hood might have were she real and in the company of an eager-beaver like himself. He told Chunk Odom, a Spec 5 in charge of the liquor-ration files at the Dak To commissary, that she had skin like expensive paper, creamy and close-pored—an organ so tight and pure it put you in mind of Philosophy and Achievement. There was a smell about her, too, Garland said. Roses, maybe, or something with vitamins in it. Spanky Morris, with the 7th in Delta

Company near Cheo Rheo, heard she had these impossible sandals and toes, to use Garland's words, of *delight* and *true daintitude*. From the grunts in Darlac province, you would've thought she was part princess, even related to several of the Mings themselves. The Hungarian ICCS delegation mentioned her in one of their communiqués.

"After a while," Garland said, "I asked her where she was going."

She showed him her ticket.

"Wyoming?" he said, shocked. "What's in Wyoming?"

She said something about heathen and made private sounds Garland took to be divinely derived.

"I was hoping she'd come with me," he told a door-gunner on a Pysops soundship once. "I said I could be a fine companion—talk, entertain when necessary, good at conserving money." But she said no, sir. Wyoming. Then rocking and rolling. Say hi, Sam the Sham and the Pharaohs. Say hi, James Brown. Throw off powers of darkness. Take up the light and shake self's tailfeathers.

Garland told a captured NVA regular that her name was Hoang Minh, something with tinkle and good feeling in it, but that she was going by Mary for the time being; and one time in '69, after Garland was gone, the name surfaced in a COM/SIT report of a radio intercept out of Duc Lap. Another time a CIA clerk found her name in a REF on one of the prisoners in the snow-white interrogation rooms in Saigon. The report said she and Garland spent the whole afternoon talking, she in speech that had lilt but no sense to it, he in the hopeful language of a kid starved for company.

"It was love," Garland told his CO once. This was in a tight spot near the Do Long bridge, all about them people going insane or passing through the flame into hell. "Honest," he said, "I felt my heart move. I'm sitting there, grinning, feeling the fittest, then crunch!, that thing just flops over." It was like combat itself, only full of release and ease instead of the pent-up. His fluids turned warm, he said, and his outlook became as generous as a Rockefeller's. "I had thoughts, too," he said. "I'm sure she could read them in my face."

They ate cheeseburgers next door at the 70–80 Truck Stop and watched the sun go down ("That was the best sunset I ever saw," he told Archie Coy, "everything since's been a disappointment!"), then she showed him a song she was writing, one which featured melancholy and trouble in the form of human thwarts but which finished with a chorus of do-do-dos that put you in mind, say, of truth and deserveds. "It was about me," he said to Archie. "There was a guy in it who was tall, which I am, and big with his spirit."

Then, at night, they the only customers in the station, she slept. "Put her head on my shoulder," he said. "Can you believe her breathing?" he said, not the Vietnam huff'n'puff of panic and wet fear, but like the strings of her nerves had loosened. "My arm was around her," he said once to an I Corps dipstick named Mayhew who didn't believe any of it. "She was tired, you could tell." Then Garland, himself overcome and deeply satisfied, fell asleep.

"I had this dream I was on the bus, the last seat back by the port-o-san." It was an old bus, he said, from the 40s or thereabouts, shaped like a bullet traveling backwards and so high you could look into the faces of passing truckers. Everybody was smoking, he said, Camels, Lucky Strikes (a guy from the Delta heard it was Pall Malls or one of them sissy smokes, like Viceroy). Outside of El Paso, this woman got on, maybe three hundred pounds, with plenty of sweat. She swayed all the way to the back, lugging a ratty suitcase, hunting a seat, and Garland knew that he was going to get up, be polite, let her have his. Which he did. She was mean-looking, he said, like maybe her mood had permanently shifted to the anger side of feeling. Like she was unwhole-someness itself breathed into life by Want and Envy.

In his dream, she was chewing Red Man, her teeth slicked like a dog's. So, he stood beside the toilet, people squeezing by to relieve themselves, him growing headachy from the road noise and smoke thick enough to drown in and the odors of dozens in close, heavy heat. It was horrible, he told an Ohio draftee at LZ Thelma, standing for hundreds of miles, a colicky baby crying up front, the driver once yelling at some guy to take his feet off the chair, that huge woman pawing through her clothes. "You didn't want to look in that suitcase," he told everybody. "It was shameful." The miles rolled on and he could see nothing outside except heat shim-mers and red dust from the flatlands and once a scrawny horse rubbing against a bent-over telephone pole. "It was a nightmare, what it was," he said, like Vietnam itself, ever-lasting and tawdry. His legs cramped and he felt greasy, his hair having lost all its youthful flair; soreness had come over him like a big net. And, after a time, he was crying himself, his diaphragm tight like a drumhead, out of breath from the bane of it all, face muscles tense and twitching, unable to stop drooling, wishing he was back somewhere in a bus station, say, with a pure beauty resting on his shoulder, being close to the life-affirming. "And when I woke up," he said, "I was."

(This was Pee Wee King's favorite part, where Garland H. Steeples jerked awake, his face spotted with sweat, expression full of alarm and despair; Pee Wee had heard the story during some 105 shelling out of II Corps and when Garland had come to this part, all the jungle outrage stopped at once—all manner of bat, bird, monkey and crawling things going without screech or howl or intelligent chirp. "It put you on the approach to something," Pee Wee told his girlfriend years later. He said he heard a million things that night, that instant: the breathing of rootwork and fruit sweating, perhaps the tick-tock of Uncle Ho's famous Longines wristwatch.)

"I slept again, of course," Garland said. But this time, when he opened his eyes, she was walking toward a bus. For a moment, he couldn't feel anything—neither air from the open door, nor tremble, nor plastic seat he was leaning against. Then, in the fumes and the light coming at him from the floor and ceiling and dirty windows, feeling hit him with a thump, fiery nerve wheels spinning in his brain. "I was hoping she'd turn around," he told an A Camp non-com. "Maybe wave, maybe come back and hug my neck. Something." But she kept going, knapsack over her shoulder, disappearing at last onto that bus, that vehicle lurching onto the highway as if the driver was withered and vile in his interiors. "It was like it didn't happen at all," he said, as if it were a poor man's wish constructed in the imagination from the common materials of need. "It was like in the movies," Garland said. "When people get off the phone, they don't say goodbye or anything. They just hang up."

Oh, he could admit later, it was a thrilling moment— fraught and prodigious. "It was like finding out you were adopted," he said, "or a switched baby." (Once, he told a Can Tho medic, there was a certain nose resemblance between himself and Mr. Henry Cabot Lodge; a certain aspect to the eye region, also.) But, mainly, he believed his was a story about luck, about being in the right place and so on, from which he developed a supremely abstruse theory involving intersecting planes and profane holiness and advanced species to be found only in special literatures, and featuring a lot of parlez-vous about numbers and where vigors come from, and how one climbs on and off another, and nameless but sanctified residues, and the quote inevitable convergence unquote which was supposed to take place when raunch gave way to uplift and heartwork became the point of all human endeavor.

She was the girl of his dreams, all right, and on the day he shipped out, neither to be seen nor heard from again, he claimed he was entering a new period in life, one of identifiable comforts and delicious viands, a thing of appetite and the means to slake it; he said bye-bye that day to fifty guys, shaking hands and kissing on the lips, finally moving toward the transport so loose and so free that it appeared to several men, among them Doyle Eugene Wingo, that Garland, falling away from the current fracas like meat from a bone, was about to take up residence in the pearly palaces of dreamland itself, him a charter citizen of an empire supported only by wish and marvel, and a near miss with love.

After he left, you heard the story often and from unlikely sorts. It was told by "Black Luigi," and appeared in the chitty-chat of GVN, the Mission and the Corsican Mafia. Edward Landsdale himself, pouring tea and whiskey in his

Saigon villa, told a Special Forces spook that it was bogus, a thing that ducked evil in favor of the big lie of fantasy. You heard it in the old headquarters of the Deuxième Bureau from a drunk Cat contractor from Des Plaines. It was heard in a New Life Village once, all the fremitus gone from it. You heard it embellished or picked clean. Were the story a plant, someone said, it would wear short-shorts and read French. Once, O. T. Winans, a Roy Acuff look-alike from Houston, heard the yarn from a Seabee who'd heard it from an Engineer in the 11th who'd heard it from those at the V-ring near CoRoc Ridge where it had been picked up by those sneaking over the Laotian border. O. T. said the story had then only hair and knobby elbow, all the hormonal elements removed, the meeting itself taking place in some rotted gook paradise, Garland no more than that oft-cited boy meeting that familiar girl and doing a thing which involved exertion and gristle that went squeak-squeak-squeak. Sometimes, Garland wasn't in it at all, his place being taken by those with an eye on the furthermore; and sometimes, he was so stripped away or made over he could be, in the same telling, tall and short, full of swank or a man with a patch over one eye and a mission cribbed from the next generation of comic book. In the Philippines, the story took an hour to tell; and once, in a place of casual death, it took many days, several of its lines muffled in the boom-boom-boom of Incoming.

Then it came back to the World. Zookie Limmer told it to his momma, it now being a property with a dozen heads and enough episodes for Metro, Goldwyn and Mayer themselves. Ellen Morris, Spanky's wife, told him to shut up after she heard, for the fifth time, that part wherein the couple performs a serious clinch, all the time making fitful animal

utterances; and Archie Coy got fired from his position as
Assistant Manager at a Kroger's for putting it on the PA, his
voice full of howl and cosmic flutter when he did the imita-
tion of the hero's love-bloated heart and the way his muscles
began snapping when the woman, now fully defined and
moving aboard a sleepy-time wave of chiffon, drifted out of
doors and into her fiery and splendid conveyance, a chorus
of celestials making an adenoidal noise of rise and virtue.

The story was told last, it appears, by Onan Motley in the
Mile 49 bar outside of Tatum to a woman named Bonnie
Suggs who kept saying, as they drove to her place in the Vista
Trailer Park, "Is that so?" or "You're fooling, Onan, ain't
you?" He was drunk, wine having soaked even the slightest
of his molecules, but he said, "No, siree, lady," lingering
over many moments, those with texture and depth, just as
he later lingered over Bonnie's tight tummy and welcoming
thighs, grabbing her tangle of hair and holding on—through
the gloomy sections, especially—trying to put himself in the
place Garland was, a discrete and illuminated landscape of
wanting love and having it.

Onan went slowly over the details of the station, spending
nearly an hour on the pinball machine which was called
Invaders and offered endless rewards based upon reflex and
greed. He showed Bonnie where the litter was, how the fluor-
escent light highlighted all the scuffs and pits in the floor tile,
where the No-Pest Strip hung and what the old codger behind the counter did with his tongue when asked a tough
question. Onan made the sounds of passing trucks, from
horn to mushy air brakes, illustrating how close the road was
and describing bird life and who came or went and how they
looked in dress or workshirt or, once, in a wash-'n'-wear suit

by J. C. Penney. Then it was over, and the two of them lay in sheet and sweat, Onan swollen with pride and thanks, almost feeling for an instant or two the shining presence of Garland himself—at that moment which may have been the high point of an entire life—underscoring the moral which he said every time his story had: a moral which was complex and finicky and a thing as fundamental as shelter, a moral, you know, which resisted all words save those which trafficked in fortune and love.

HAVING THE HUMAN THING OF JOY

In the no-account crossroads I grew up in—Deming, New Mexico—I supposed that love was the usual force of jackpot and despair; and I supposed further, as a youngster, that love for my parents—and surely all adults!—was not a fairy tale, as I have discovered, of fleshes and sweats, but was what my wife Vicki once called a "food-gathering enterprise with taxes and child-rearing thrown in." Parents, those Misters and Missuses who whomped you and told you when to brush, were, I thought, just taller versions of children themselves: hairier, stronger of breath and limb, familiar with the exotic dangers of, say, war and faraway places. They were a kind, an ignorant kid believed, as different (and alike) as the reptile and the bird. They didn't live where we did, in a world only of tragedy and hysteria; their pleasures were meaner, less durable; their sorrows light as cotton, swept away by an easy deed or a single word. They were giants, yes, and in the time I am writing about they were giants without fear or wonder, without desires and frustrations from them.

My mother (about whom this partly is) was merely that figure who floated about our house in one of a thousand hats—of straw and felt and fabrics we moderns have lost track of, some with feathers or ribbons or veils, all wide-brimmed and of course floppy. Actually, as she is now dead several years and I was out of her house as a teenager, I find I remember little else about her. She was a gardener, I believe, and liked to read books like *Love Is My Stranger* (which, when I looked it up, concerned misery and the surprise it is). She enjoyed cooking and once she dressed up like an elf for the Xmas I got my Lionel Flyer train, but I had no sense of her as a woman, what my used-to-be best friend Buster Meeks says is a common creature of gland and habit. Inconceivable as you know it is, she had nothing in common with what you can find in any drugstore nowadays: which is female fetched up in leather or well foamed from a shower, the whole of her moist and heedless, without spirit or moral faculty. As far as I was concerned, Mother was the person, cranky and intolerant, who fed me; or she was the white-haired person, aged and shortsighted and quiet as a hermit, who'd lived with us for a short time until her death; nothing in between.

There is little about her funeral you need to know except that it was hot with the sunshine we brag about and over-long, with much from Dr. Tippit (the collegiate Episcopalian whose flock we are) about reward and promise in the after-world. The only people who cried were my boys, Taylor and Buddy, and they more from the quiet and the frightful black-ness of our outfits; and then we all came home in my Biscayne. We were closemouthed, very impressed by death and the ceremony surrounding it, and we spent the rest of that Saturday afternoon moving about on tiptoes, waiting perhaps for sundown or a rainstorm to wash away the feelings we were expected to have. It was probably Taylor, the hottempered one, who started it, who freed us to be the loud bunch we are, and I think he did it by slugging Buddy on the earhole or wanting dinner. In any case, there was an hour of shouting and some ordering about from Vicki and me, food appeared and we ate, the TV going in the family room, and then this woman I married, herself a practical person, said I ought to go into my mother's room and begin sorting junk from keepsake, the former of which we could donate or pitch out.

Widowed a long time (my daddy having died of a heart attack many years ago), Mother had made her room a virtual temple of knick knack and sentimental curio. Needlepoint was her principal endeavor, a craft she had taken up with the industry of a coolie. She could do anything: poodle dog, master of art like Picasso, sayings meant to touch your tearful nature like "Bless this hearth ..." and "This Be the Verse." She had saved, it appeared, everything—cocktail napkin from the Rustler in Phoenix, dancecard from a cruise they once took to Panama, my daddy's birth certificate (which showed him to be Texan and white); and the atmosphere of the room was that which belongs to old ladies everywhere: cozy with clutter arranged in piles and airborne a smell which was part dusty geegaw (a word I learned from her), part wilted flora. What struck me most was the sense that there had been nothing in her life—neither event, nor notion, nor fleeting feeling—which had not been recorded, made real as history.

For a time I sat, overwhelmed and partly reluctant; then I did as I'd been instructed. I carried out her plant life first, the ferns and cacti and potted growth she'd spent maybe two hundred dollars for at Woolworth's. I took down some pictures: of my daddy standing in front of the Chevrolet dealership he bought in '56; of the two of them dressed Hawaiian for a night at the Mimbres Valley Country Club; of her alone, in a hat made notorious by Lady Astor, swinging a golf club. She had clothes, too—as many as you might expect to find in the closets of those who rule, say, Siam or another kingdom where it is a crime to wear the same suit twice. There were dresses which looked Spanish and pants I believe they used to call Capri (or toreador), plus wraps with more sparkle and twinkle than nighttime. Once I called Vicki in and asked if she wanted any of the shoes. "Good God, Lamar," she said, "look at those things." They seemed quaint, I'll admit, mostly dark and some with heels which could be used for hammering into soft woods. "Go on," I said, "try one on." And she did, scowling a bit then grinning when one pair, shiny as patent, fit as if she'd bought them yesterday. "What do you think?" Vicki said, and for an instant she looked as she had years ago when I met her at SMU. "I'll keep these," she said. (She was a psychology major and believes, even now, in making up your mind fast, without the hemming and hawing you see in those who prefer to be coaxed.)

I worked until ten, I remember, then watched the Channel 9 news (KTSM) to know about the world we lived in. There was small talk, some yelling at the dingleberry Mr. Ford was, then we went into our bedroom where Vicki pulled off her shirt and grabbed me. "Maybe it isn't appropriate," she said, "but I want you to fill me up right now." I was not in grief and she was, as is said in many popular songs, life. "You know me," she said, "I got to have it when I got to have it." The next morning, I woke early and went to work in Mother's room again without waking anybody. In my dreams I had seen myself as I was—thirty-six years old, an educated man with some property, a member for a time of Kiwanis, and proud of little more than the upright sort I was. I re-member being happy that morning, not mournful as many get, and worked the way you see old-timers do, as if with a plan and at a reasonable pace. I was slowed only by the trunks, of which there were two, and the hundreds and hundreds of photographs they contained. These photo-graphs, it seemed, had come from a different world, one which lacked the conveniences and aggravations of the cur-rent life. Only a few in color, they showed my daddy in England (he had been a soldier, involved in what he called "the underground balloon corps"), and my mother with her people in Louisiana, and fat-bottomed relatives named Ike and Uncle Inches and Carroll, plus such friends as Maizie and Al and the Zants (Royce and Irene). My mother wore the hats she was famous for, on the beaches and even in front of Mr. Lincoln's statue in Washington, hats with the swoop and roll another might call almost epic. On the back of one picture was this message: "All these people are dead, I don't know where"; and on another, this of my granny, in Mother's own hand, was this: "She was angry this day and Fletcher had to drag her out for this pose." It was a life I was seeing—of homes I'd never slept in, folks I'd never shake hands with, of monuments I hadn't stood in front of or complained about visiting. For an hour or so, fascinated, I picked through those curled and smudged things, puzzled as an infant; then I came to the one you know I'm here to tell about.

Artfully crisscrossed by shadow, it was a picture of a woman standing with her back to the camera, her pointy chin tilted up and to the right; skin as white as paper, she was, except for her shoes and stockings, very and profoundly naked. You could see some thigh, slender but not weak-looking, and the tuck of an ass young boys still would go crazy over, plus wings which were shoulder blades and, around the knuckles of her spine, muscles you knew were still tight as new rope. I believe now I heard that wise guy's voice which is said to be inside us, and it was saying, "Be prepared, Lamar." I must've held the thing for a minute before I noticed the hand which was reaching toward her from out of the frame (the hand of the photographer!). I could feel the whole house then, as if it were a living creature, grow still. "Who is this?" I said and, at the moment I heard Vicki getting up next door, I knew, for I could see on that outstretched hand a ring familiar to me as my own face. The little voice was silent. I felt a click in the forehead and a heavy lurch in my chest, as if I held a thumping heart in my fist. I knew that the fingers reaching forward, as if to caress, belonged to the giant who was my father and the woman, nude and lovely and real as death itself, was the other giant whose life I did not know, my mother.

This is one story I tell and until yesterday I believed it was only about growing up and how it is to shed the life-dumb youngster you are. I believed its medium was movie-time shock and it meant to stir you by saying, in effect, "Welcome into the dark world of grown-up animals." It was disconnected, I believed, not like other disturbances I might have. I thought, if I may be poetic, it stood out there in the landscape of my life the way the Pyramids do—something done once and astounding for it. I have seen it written in a storybook Buddy has that life is a train ride, with many stations and much clickety-clack—which, though it is only metaphor, may be true; but the ride is not straight because every now and then—as between one event and another—it is revealed, so the book says, that quote you are making a curve and a light is thrown back showing a mountain of meaning rising behind you on the way you've come unquote.

Yesterday, years from the time I saw that picture of my mother, it was revealed to me that Vickie was seeing another man. I found this note on my windshield when I was ready to come home: *Lamar T. Hoyt, your wife is having relations with Buster Meeks. I saw them today and she was hollering, "Fill me up, God damn you, go ahead and do it."* It was that moment found in many movies these days: revelation of the dire kind, swift as if from God, the moment in which the gent you're rooting for sees that he is neither good nor able but weak with a rascal's needs, average as a dollar bill. Yet, for a second, I was not breathless or slumped in the brain. Then it came, and I was stunned, for I suddenly saw—yes, as if I were looking at another picture—the Vicki I knew; she was naked and slapping herself atop skinny Buster Meeks, sharing with him the jubilation and outcries I thought were mine. There, standing beside my pickup, the whole of my meager municipality quitting its trades and businesses to go home to be fed, I saw my straight-talking spouse as just another being on this dark planet—female and driven by common, ancient desires. She was not merely wife, as Mother had not been merely Mother, but Vicki was there, in Buster's rattly sedan, human and having the human thing of joy.

And next, for the first time in years, I thought of that morning I found the Kodak. I had tried working for a little while but couldn't, being drawn to that grainy photograph as a drunk is drawn to more drink. Then, about the time Vicki said breakfast was ready, wash up, I left that room to sit out on the patio near the hole which was the pool we were building. You could see the scrub-covered hills in the distance, lit up and large the way they are in dreamland. The picture in my pocket, I was having the kind of thoughts a fish might have; something would come to mind, slight and insubstantial but with a face, and then be gone. I could hear Buddy and Taylor squabbling and, next door, Hal Thibodeaux cussing out his new lawn mower. Above was high heaven, blue and vast as time; below was earth I owned; and between them, me, full of new knowledge but unable to speak it. "Lamar," Vicki was saying from the glass door, "what in hell's wrong with you?" She was wearing shorts and had legs which always brought out the touching part of me. "You'd better eat now," she said, "I'm going to the Club this afternoon." So I got up then, old-timey picture hidden, and said, "Come with me" and led her back to our room. Her hands have the finest tiny veins in the world and I stroked them for a time before saying, "Vicki, I want you to put your arms around me and just hold." She looked confused, as if I'd asked for Congo Zulu from her, but almost immediately she grabbed on as I'd hoped she would. "Tighter," I said. She had the squeeze of a farm girl, a profound act which involves concentration and knowledge of the tender parts. "When do I get to let go?" she said. I had my head on her neck and could smell the thing we'd done last night, plus what the pores had added. "I'll tell you when," I said. For a long time I stayed pressed against her as I had once stayed pressed against another, and for that time, which I could hear moving by as a heartbeat, I wasn't me any longer: I was someone small and helpless and comforted as a child.

I felt the same yesterday when I stuffed that note in my glove box, in there with the Shell charge tickets and other wastepaper I mean to clean out tomorrow. "Okay," I said to my steering wheel, "I'll have me a drink when I get home." I had the window down so I could hang my arm out like a casual man. "I'll watch some TV or maybe wrestle with Buddy." I had an ordinary citizen's voice, clear and from the chest. Then I said this: "If it's a ride we're on, I'm the one looking down and away; don't turn my face to the mountains and such you see." In the west, where hope is said to lie, clouds were piling up, gray and pink and yellow, air upon air upon air. "I want to be blind," I said. "I want my train ride to be long and flat," I said. "I don't want to see what's rising behind me," I said.

And then I was home.

THE UNFINISHED BUSINESS
OF CHILDHOOD

I

Before they became our national sensation, Bobby Stoops
billed his rock and rollers as The Feet of Yemen, a contrary
and twice-mad group that sang of the Condition: "It is hell,"
he told an audience one night, "I can't wait to get back."
During this period, he was Dr. Filth, what the skinny writer
from *Musician* called a "juiced-up fag-out of mock murder;
the wrecked specter fathers fear most." Later, he became
Dwana Lynne Cootey, country girl, and made his hair shoot
up like a wheat field. Other times, he was a state of mind—
disquiet, want, Lutheranism—a thought upright, with ankle
and mouth; and his group became The Dogs of New Jersey,
More Facts About Beavers and Wet Places at Noon.

"I put it to you this way," his manager, Putt Fenno, said

finally. "In Arkansas, you have no fans, only confusion. They have mistaken you for a conifer." Fenno himself looked like a two-hundred-pound tool box. "Stop breaking my neck. Give me something I can peddle to Finns."

So, during those months their records remained on *Billboard*'s Top 40, and until Bobby menaced that teenage woman in the Cleveland Agora, they were The Eldest of Things, he the frontmost of a fivesome that played "I Want It All" and "Kill the Rich/Eat the Poor." These were tunes, he told the *Times-Herald,* that seized belligerence to make it toil for the dispossessed.

Eventually, in a way he would one day understand as inevitable, Bobby developed contempt for the whole process. "I have a dark place in me," he told Putt Fenno. "The light of love does not reach." At the Palamino in North Hollywood, he called the crowd cowards, simpletons. "The principal enemy of art is fame," he said. He could hear a woman in the back screeching: "Shove it in here, Dimitri! I want to swell up like a Turk." Once, hours late for a session at the Record Plant, he ate a thousand-dollar bill. "I would only spend it on myself," he told his bass player, Nate Creer. "I would still be sad." On Quaaludes, he carried a Vestin-M .38, a nastiness which he pointed at everybody; on speed, he taped a filet knife to his leg and made Putt Fenno weep.

"It is an odd life," he confessed to a reporter, "a march from one desire to the next."

In the end, the months ran together until, while performing miraculous figures on his Fender that night in Cleveland, he saw nothing left for himself but reckless despair. During "Lesser Stars We Shine Among," he spotted her at the edge of the stage, her face bright with rapture. "Come to me," he said, "I am empty inside." In the wings, Putt Fenno had the look of a man with many debts. "I am to make a statement," Bobby shouted over the PA. The girl stood beside him, thirsty as an adder. She represented them all, he told the crowd that night—the drossy, the fevered, the displaced, all of us who'd lost our way in the brillig, tulgey wood. "I am here to make a statement," he hollered. There was a howl of feedback. Eyes ablaze, he informed them that his was an immodest rearguard action in the service of, well, in the service of goodness—said action to be dispensed by this thing here, which was an ugly bone-handled skinning blade, said service to be performed by driving his point right smack into the thumping, sticky center of her, and our, plight.

"Forgive me," he said, "large times demand large gestures."

He hadn't cut her, it developed, but there was undesired publicity, expensive attorneys and a weekend in the Justice Center holding tank.

"Let us welcome you," one prisoner said, and four others, all heavily scarred black men in shower caps and Aunt Pecos hair curlers, bounded to their feet. They could have been a group themselves, one whose themes were morphinism and pox.

Said one: "I have sampled the treasures of Safeway and J. C. Penney; ain't nothing compares to the sweets of Miss Laticia."

Said a second: "Pray with us, white boy, that we might go forth and burgle."

That Monday, the judge lectured Bobby for half an hour. "Perhaps you have heard of me, as well," he said, his face that of a darksome animal. "Years ago, I wrestled under the name The Love of Britomart. I once tangled with the immortal Augustine Crespi of Argentina. In Public Hall, we went many rounds in a tropical heat. He had the growl, I the nimble feet. In the seventh, he pulled a trowel from his shorts. I was disheartened. Now, with similar enthusiasm, I battle perfidy."

Bobby felt a muscle let go in his chest. "I am a battler, too," he said. "I stand against dirty talk and self-neglect. Let's do this together, your judgeship. You can be the bow, I the lilting lyre."

The judge leveled a finger at him. He appeared to be having slanderous thoughts.

"Go away, defendant Stoops. I am feeling the call of the spinning toe-hold."

"You disappoint me," Putt Fenno told him at the Greyhound station. "We had possibilities. I saw us in a Swiss vault, bathing in coin. I was fond of you, too. Now, I'm off—what?—to make fruit famous."

For twenty-six hours, Bobby rode, slumped in his seat. He looked at his hand. It could have belonged to a sloth, his heart to a lizard. With every mile, he felt less like that celebrated outlaw he'd been for so long; and by the time the bus pulled into Deming, New Mexico, he knew that for a long time—six years, it would turn out—he would neither be the Night Crawler, nor the Wicked Dwarf of the Western Shore, nor another demon from the nether quarters of his undermind.

"Shake this hand," he told the driver as he got off. "This belongs to Bobby Stoops and he has a lifetime to figure out how to tell the world what is wrong with it."

He rented an apartment on Olive Street, a dozen blocks from his mother and father, and worked at Buzz King's Chevron on US 70; in time, no one remembered he was the fellow who'd sung "Sick Figure in the Neighborhood" or "Old Fool Back on Earth," or that at the Park West in Chicago he'd spoken of the Tattooers of La Dominica and The Order of the Golden Dawn. Only once was he recognized, by Onan Motley, the kid who worked the pumps.

"I know Experiment in India." Onan looked like he had fist in his throat. "I know Datalife." He hummed the bridge in which the shoo-bops sound like an army in retreat.

Bobby Stoops was not encouraged.

"I am an ex-ag major from Texas Tech," Bobby said. Covered in bearing grease from a California Ford LTD, he felt no more like his former self than he did gravel. "Perhaps you'd care to know details about the swamp potato. Or lichen."

"I was in II Corps then," Onan was saying. "You were heavy shit to a lot of us. We'd put on 'Orders for the Library' and rock out with Victor Charles. It was bullets and LZ Thelma. I liked best that thing you called forethought."

"I know you," Bobby said, "you are interested in moss and phytogenesis."

"I used to be a bad character." Motley was serious. "You turned me toward the good path."

In the spring, Bobby discovered he was a legend. He'd been seen, it was reported, in Cambodia with a Communist combo called Modern Slavery. They sang "Let's Play Under the Bed" and "Important Moments in the History of Russia," and for state engagements they dressed up like KGB samaritans named Roxy and Do Ling. One publication—

was it *Circus*?—claimed that, in his first week as sheriff of Brownfield, Texas, he had vanquished a felon while speaking Jacobean. "Hark, ye motherfucker," he reportedly had ordered, "little availeth. Unhand that purloined raiment!" The article suggested he was feral, with a heart as insubordinate as lighting. An old picture (the one to promote "Stockings That Think") appeared on the *Newsweek* people page. The paragraph below it, Bobby was sure, was written by an iguana, for it spoke of a "constricted world of misgivings" in which "beings such as he tempted beings such as us into the worship of tumult and shudder."

He liked living in New Mexico, especially its desert. "Greatness could happen here," he told Buzz King. This was a place, he decided, like his past: scorched, flat and unremarkable but for its twisted, gnarled and needled plant life. (During this time—from Easter '74 to Xmas '78—he began developing himself. He bowled at the Thunderbird Lanes, found he could do it well, even liked it. He received permission from the Wildcat wrestling coach to use the weight room and there he exercised three times a week, doing ten reps for the major muscle groups—the flexors, the extensors, even Gimbernat's ligament.) Yet, when he thought about the past, he felt dazed, as if his thinking meats had suddenly dried, had fractured and now were already crumbling along the fissure of Rolando; and once the coach caught him with 180 pounds braced over his head—he'd been that way for an hour, it appeared. The man said Bobby's eyes seemed, well, to drift in his face.

"You take it easy," the coach suggested. "Skip a week, then start again. But small this time. You ain't no Hercules."

"Right, sure," Bobby said. There was nothing in his brain but wind and light.

Somewhere in here he married, but even after the climactic WJKO speech and the complete return to the normal life, which were both many years away, he remembered little more than her name, Evelyn Greathouse, and that she was the ER nurse at the Mimbres Valley Hospital who bandaged the wrist he'd whanged with a tire iron. He did recall that she was pretty—as few seemed to be—and that one week they drove south to Las Palomas, were wedded by a Mexican JP and bebopped at Tillie's, on the juke box his record that had gone to number four, "Instantly Jealous of Grain." She lived in the Olive Street apartment for many months and wore a perfume called White Shoulders, and then she was gone: for all her skill in the healing arts, she'd been too interested in that difficult, absent creature he'd been, that one who had sung to us in the big world about disorder, swill and common trespass.

II

One day, while he nailed new roofing felt on his garage, he heard talk. It was that comic-strip scene of self-illumination: light bulb overhead, a way to save the world, the problem solved. With a start, he realized that, despite the frenzy of those early years, he hadn't yet said what needed saying. "I did not state it as Victor Fears," he allowed. "Nor in Black Music From Two Worlds. Nor as Men Without Rhyme."

At the horizon the sun appeared tilted at a peculiar angle. The desert shimmered, heat waves everywhere and rising, an empire of thunderclouds tumbling toward him. He had his shirt off, his hands black with roofing tar, stomach slick with sweat. Titles came to him: *Daughters of Rich Men, We Destroy the Family;* and, in the middle distances, a picture of himself emerged, shining and uninvaded. He could smell something, too, like new earth—soil from the vacated marl of accomplishment.

"I mean to swell up and bristle," he whispered. "I mean to scold."

An hour later he had sent telegrams to *Rolling Stone,* to *Tiger Beat,* to the *Village Voice*—to all the press that had followed his career. "Mr. Stoops's exile is ended," the messages read. "He has recovered himself and seeks now to pass along his ideas. P.S. You may not recognize him now as he is bald and affects the aspect of a haunted man."

The following Saturday, Bobby greeted a writer-photographer from the *Trouser Press.*

"I have missed the spotlights," Bobby said. "And the way trouble looks from the high road." He made muscles to demonstrate that a new spirit had entered his body, as well as his mind.

The man had the penmanship of a Goth. The article, when it appeared, asserted that Bobby had uttered Iroquois. There were allusions to lodge poles and beaded wampum.

"Attend to your latter ends," Bobby said. "For example, the end of mirth is heaviness."

The fellow snapped a photo which showed Bobby with a torso firm as a tusk.

"Fierce wars and faithful loves shall moralize my songs." Bobby was looking into the man's eys. There were flecks in the iris that could have been produced only by amphetamines. "I suspect I will be vast, and a mighty turmoil to the ignorant many."

Until he heard from Putt Fenno, Bobby practiced hard, delighted in his expert fingerwork, the way he caressed the fretboard. "Digits," he said, "you have lost nothing but time." His voice, too, had remained in splendid shape—still able, when he needed it, to wail and cause the blood to tremble. He told his mother and father that they were not to worry, that he would be leaving soon, but would one day return to them, a risen and everlasting thing. He informed the Wildcat coach that he no longer had need of iron and inert flange, but the ache of exertion had made him appreciate the physical world of tendon, joint and bone. On his last day of work at Buzz King's he told the kid who'd recognized him that several paths existed in this life, not one or two, and that down all, dale or slough, jungle or avenue, lay miracle and tragedy both—the fudged and deprived, respectively.

"Yeah, I heard that before." Onan Motley's face—gaunt and held together, it seemed, by hope alone—grew dark, as if he'd spied a hairy item with a dozen legs dart from the dirt at his feet. "Our CO, Captain Fooley, used to say that just after we got dumped on. He'd stroll out on the char, where the smoke and screaming was coming from, and say, 'Men, ain't life lovely?' I didn't believe it then."

Bobby grabbed Onan by the shoulders, planted a saint's kiss on the boy's gritty forehead.

"Bless you," he said. "You are from rancor and clatter, and all shall be over soon."

His return, as expected, was swift. At LAX, in the breath-defeated embrace of Putt Fenno, Bobby spoke the three words that had seized his thoughts since he'd boarded the AA flight in El Paso: blight, spoilage, mendacity.

"I have no humor left in me," Putt Fenno said. "Listen, you must agree to the following. You may not batter, maim, or slap around. You may not shoot, stab, pummel or cold-cock. I have sent your luggage back. There was a bazooka in it."

Bobby glanced at the document Putt Fenno was holding. It forbade the use of anything manufactured by Uzi or Messrs. Smith & Wesson. It forbade reference to catamites or Tyuratum vertebrates. It disallowed anaphraxis and sleep standing up.

"I feel a hundred years old," Putt Fenno was saying. "Make us rich again, okay?"

Bobby grinned. More words had occurred and he wondered if there was a tune among them: filament, continence, ghastly.

"Hug me again," Fenno said. "It's been a long time since I drank for pleasure."

After a month's rehearsal in a warehouse off Los Feliz Boulevard, the band began a six-date tour, starting in Tampa, as The Unfinished Business of Childhood. "It is good," Bobby told the crowd that first night. He had concluded "Lunch in Tunisia," the hall glowing with a million sparkles. "It will get better: the point of evolution is perfection. In time you will twinkle and glitter above." He saw, in the back, a legion of Spanish pirates and dispersed Apaches. They had skin the color of week-old pork. "Ease your pain," he told them, and, almost a hundred strong, eyes aglow with what Bobby knew were ardors and mordancies, they lurched forward. Bobby was touched, as if in them, in the smokes and swirling lights, he had glimpsed parts of himself—the hungry, condemned parts.

"Larger spirits are using me," he told Putt Fenno after the show. He was dressed in a velveteen jumpsuit, the ensemble that had made hair fashionable several seasons ago. "To-morrow night, I shall shower them with fur."

"I have a confession." In Fenno's face was something like pain. "I have an ulcer. My ears ring all the time. Be nice to me."

Across the room, Nate Creer, the bass player, was wooing a woman. Bobby could read his lips: he was discussing, in the context of the discarnate, humbug and pluck.

"I am writing a new tune," Bobby said. "It is called 'Yonder Wall in Japan' and suggests ruin."

The following night, after the performance in Birmingham, he found a surprise in his hotel. They were, he figured, heathen—on account of their breastplates and appealing smiles, not to mention exposed, muscular thighs. This, evidently, was to be that male-female principle he'd read much about.

"I have hitched many miles," the brunette was saying, "show me something vile." She was taller and had a reptile's lip curl Bobby found fascinating. The other was blonde, clearly from the Triassic age. Bobby envisioned a man, like himself, in climbing boots and leathers, adrool astride them, the welts on his pectorals those of combat and extirpation. He showed them the bed, which seemed as large now as a great white sea, and they dashed to it in a style Bobby took to be species-specific. In a moment, all was flurry and a thunderclap of peeled outerware. A thought, obvious as a brick, struck him: If I can have this, why am I not happy?

"Now we will demonstrate the difference between curiosity and interest," a voice from the pile said. "You may ask questions later."

Reckless as a nightmare, they roiled, bed linen flying, at

once a huddle and a tempest. He found them amazing, like poultry that could fox-trot and add by twos. For a time, he sat on the coffee table, watchful as a sentry. A garment, heavy with buckles and bows, flopped over the table lamp. Another song occurred to him: *All About the Whites.* He saw hank and thatch and a certain square of skin that could have belonged to either. "Ah, wretchedness," the blonde was groaning. "Ah, excess," sighed the brunette, eyeballs rolling. His heart virtually frozen, Bobby saw tongue and root and, after an hour, a flank of such delectation his lungs withered with a wheeze.

"We are lonely," the brunette declared. "Help us into the upper airs."

Bobby made his leg stop shaking. "What is your name?"

"Suzy," she said. "Though I am often known as Hellenora. Or Florimel."

"Yes, I have heard of you."

There was a profound instant, itself bittersweet as nightshade, during which Suzy studied the breathless sprawl of flesh beneath her. It moaned of ecstasy and a work of nature called Chaco.

"This is Adele," Suzy said. "Many claim she invented shelter."

In Atlanta the next day, after the load-in and the sound check, Bobby told Putt Fenno he was going for a ride, visit the landmarks. "I have received a message." He'd spotted a sentence on the wall in his dressing room, its letters bunched and clumped, as if etched with an adze. "I am to venture among them. Ideas are surfacing. There are rumors of exuberance and enmity."

"I have an idea, too. It involves retirement comforts," Putt Fenno said. "What's that sound?"

"My liver," Bobby said.

Putt Fenno's eyes snapped out of focus, came back. "Convince me. I am skeptical."

"It is Greek," Bobby said. "I believe it endeavors to be free and live on a verdant isle."

All afternoon, warmed by a strangely Persian sun, he toured Atlanta, from Washington Park to Georgia Tech and Peachtree Center, his silver Cadillac limousine driven by a man whose face brought to Bobby's mind the terms *figwort* and *thermocline*.

"You have suffered a recent loss," Bobby said at last.

"Ain't that the goddamn truth."

The car pulled onto Chapel Street, near Terminal Station.

"It involves a woman," Bobby added, "and an ex–New Orleans banker named Fudge."

The man looked like a broke farmer in receipt of yet more bad news.

"Her name is Lou Ann, from the house of Akers," Bobby said. "Yours is—"

"Al. Alfred, " he said, "from the, uh, house of Boozer."

"Cheer up, Alfred Boozer." Bobby clapped him on the shoulder. It felt like stone. "They are an inconstant pair. This minute they squabble in a Cobb County bungalow. She holds a stick, he a tennis sock. They are discussing the pineal body and what to do with unnecessary fibrous matter." Bobby felt removed from this, as if he'd come from another, less-complicated orb. "Yearning for a glamorous career, she has dyed her hair henna; he, alas, comes from a tribe which used to compute in yods."

"He's an investment broker with a five-thousand-dollar Rolex, is what he is." Alfred Boozer had the car stopped in the street. "Lou Ann says he's got a heinie like a teenager."

Bobby was pleased he'd worn this Arab costume—these robes, this warrior's burnoose.

"At this moment Lou Ann is seminaked but dismal in her mind. Where they are, it has rained for the seventh time in as many days; and last night she saw the rusted hulk of an Oldsmobile wagon tumble past on the nasty river behind their dwelling." Cars were honking, a knot of motorists waving. "She is holding herself at the bosom. Where I come from, we call these features glomerules; often they can be the source of our strength."

"My source is George Dickel and Four Roses," Alfred Boozer was saying. "The house of Boozer's a grim joint."

It was then, while he informed Mr. Boozer of his woman's affection for benthic fauna, that Bobby noticed they were parked in front of a pawn shop. Innards, he thought, be still.

"Wait here," he said, opening his door. A voice could be heard—his own perhaps after centuries of sleep: *Robert Virgil Stoops, this is why you have come.*

"Tell me about Fudge," Alfred was hollering. "Is he standing or does he have his fist up his wazoo?"

Inside, Bobby approached the woman behind the cash register. She had wet lips, the air around her as special as blood. "Madam, you have what I need. Please, take my monies." In a few seconds, he sat again in the Cadillac, now clutching a heavy paper sack. He felt calm, none of his organs in riot. He could have been at the North Pole, alone except for expansive plains of white and a rhapsody of Arctic night noise.

"That woman spit on you." Alfred Boozer, his face wrinkled as a prune, was pointing. "What'd you buy?"

Bobby held the bag aloft. It contained a .44 with six WCF cartridges and possessed the heft, Bobby thought, of a thousand things.

"In my homeland," he said, "this is an instrument of peace, a speedy exit from the hollow world."

III

That night, Bobby Stoops, once known as Dr. Filth, a maker of statements, formerly of the American deserts, flew. During "Themes From Great Cities," in the chorus where the Pakistani finger cymbals are clinked to imitate icy, tinkling rains, Bobby felt himself harden in a dozen spots—calf, hips, small of back; then, stiffened by the thump and amplified thwang behind him, he rose. An inch. Finally two.

Nearby, mouth set hard as a doorknob, stood Nate Creer, pumping his bass feverishly. He'd been to Baylor, a physics major with several hours in Aquinas.

"Be watchful, Mr. Creer," Bobby said. "Three weeks from now you will pass from one medium to the next. I see the letters ICU, plus a flock of grave men in smocks."

Creer edged closer, adrift in the music. They were in the section that mentioned The Lip of Truth, The Froward Tongue.

"Observe," Bobby said, "I am risen. Verily."

"Right on," Nate agreed. "We are all risen in this venue. It's the pharmaceuticals."

Bobby felt sorrow clunk in him like a weight. "Give me your hand, Nathaniel, and let us shuffle together."

Afterward, backstage, amid a milling crowd of crew and

well-wishers, Bobby stared into the littered bottom of his handbag. He cocked his head and all the objects in his vision—all the objects in his life, it seemed—were at the far end of this room. He felt remarkable, like a boxer dog wearing eyeshadow and Lady Astor's rubies. "Rejoice in the habitable reaches of this earth," he said to himself. "Hear my instructions and be wise."

Putt Fenno, his face like the floor of a horsebarn, approached.

"About that radio interview in Miami tomorrow—" he began.

"My friend, you look wretched," Bobby said. "I prescribe the high road of reason, plus yellow vegetables."

Nearby, Bobby's drummer, Wang-chi, was giving his real name. It was composed of c's and x's and possessed a primitive association with jaculation.

"Let me impress you," Putt Fenno was saying. "It is our understanding that the Pope will be listening. Also, tapes are being made for Fidel's boys. You have an international following."

"Trust me," Bobby said. "I already have an outfit in mind: It will say sleek and travel in the outer darkness."

Before he slept, hovering above the bed, Bobby entertained a vision. Images of fire rolled overhead, as well as scenes of salvation. He saw unbridled steeds, ears flattened, running free amid the collapse of a crystal empire. In another, a fallen creature in gypsy headgear yelled of polymorphs and misogyny. In the last, almost familiar, a universe of eight dimensions, including the glandular, dissolved into itself and became, he knew, a grain of blackness as dense as a tear. Cold, his spine knocking, Bobby tugged the blanket to his chin.

"Ours is a mutable kind," he said. "We believe in naught but a future of joy."

In the morning, he dressed slowly. He desired a mytho-lyrical effect. In the mirror, he saw himself in a green Lycra bodysuit, the pistol in the red plastic box strapped to his chest.

"My astro-pack," he told everyone aboard the charter jet. "Today will one of irreducible mysteries and some flitting about."

Airborne, he spoke of greenswards and leafy ensconce-ments, Phoebus and enswarmed furies. "We should be think-ing of Keats and the fourth realm of space," he said over the intercom. "Not needments and habits that made us blue."

In the charter terminal, he addressed dozens of his fans. "Bobby Stoops has been away too long," he said. "But he has learned much. For example, he has learned that ma-chines have a dark and sly plan for us all. The question is this: 'What is to be done with the delirious among us, the floccose?' " Putt Fenno made him quit when the talk turned to occultism, particularly a belief in woody tissues.

At the radio station, WJKO, he was introduced to a disc jockey who wore a T-shirt which said "Resist All Change."

"Yes, I have met you before," Bobby said. "You were riding with Cortez. You were called, I believe, Bernal of Almeria."

"Buenos dias," the man laughed, ushering Bobby into a studio. "I am Xavier Mendoza Gonzalez-Boit. You may call me Jake." He was Cuban, with a floppy hairpiece, and had the shine of a man making sixty thousand dollars a year. "We are gigante," he was saying. "We got waves going all around whole world. You mas big, too. All day long phones ring. It is Stoops, Stoops, Stoops. Everybody adores hombres who fly."

In the tiny room with them paced Putt Fenno, his tie undone and collar open. He had the stuffed expression of a bottom-feeding sea fish.

"You have been hopeless too long," Bobby said to him. "I shall give you something to glimmer for."

Jake was fiddling with a bank of dials. He adjusted the boom mike. "That light turns rojo, we are go for blastoff." Above a glass panel was the fixture. "Listo?"

Bobby felt the pistol against his ribs. His thoughts, gay and light, concerned recompense and the useful charms of the past. Within minutes, he knew, this episode in his life would be over.

"I am ready, my son."

The light flashed on and Jake rushed into extended remarks that cited tierra, viento y fuego—earth, wind and fire. He was mucho honored, he said, to have this numero uno rock-'n'-roll hombre on his show. It was a thrill, muchachos, like maybe having El Presidente himself or Old Senor Elvis. "Right now this gringo is touching my cabeza and I am feeling hot stuff go up my spine."

The room, Bobby, imagined, except for the sluggish thud of his heart, was quiet. On the other side of the glass wall, people were busy, many smiling. Children, he was thinking, come unto me. I am neither sinister nor a member of low estates. Then he heard himself speaking, his voice music itself.

"My true name is Jor-El and I come from the planet Alderon, which lies outside what you know as the Vega galaxy."

There was light, blinding as from a flashbulb, and acrid smoke. It seemed he had fired the pistol into the ceiling tiles. Debris fell in a blizzard.

"Do not be alarmed, citizens of earth," he said. "This is perturbation only, not violence."

Jack had cast himself into a corner, his hair in a lump in his lap. "Carumba!" he was shouting. The good humor had vanished from his face in a flash. In the adjacent studio, folks shook in spasms, as if they had been touched, however briefly, by an electric wand.

Somewhere, Putt Fenno was blubbering.

"We are discreet people, tall and lean of build. Our fortunes, which we have no interest in hoarding, are made in the export of gummy exhudates. We talk of heths and locomote using an energy we measure in fardads. In our mountains, which resemble your Rockies in composition, we mine a mineral precious to us as the erg or dyne. Courtship in our world is without anxiety—in part because we subscribe to the wonderments of the temporary pleasures. Individuals have stepped forward to lead us in this enterprise and we consult them daily."

Jake, all Jolson eyes and kidney sweat, went many directions at once. The pistol had gone off again.

"Years ago, it was determined to make contact with you. I was selected as an infant and fitted into a uniquely designed vehicle. This was parsecs ago—three hundred years by your calendar. My transport landed in the New Mexico desert and I was taken in by the Stoops family, beautician Mildred and plumber Earl. Living among you as a scholar, I have learned your language and can use with confidence the words *gout* and *epicene*. I have eaten your foods and found them chewy. Your cities I enjoy very much, though they lack the splash and gleam of our capital, El-Dor. My mission is simple: I bring you greetings and counsel from our Circle of Elders."

In his corner, Jake was striking himself in an alarmingly private manner. "Holy mother," he was saying, "holy mother."

Putt Fenno, his eyes blank with panic, was collapsed on the floor.

"I have information about betterments," Bobby was saying. "The details will make you frolic and gambol."

The ceiling moved, and Bobby felt a comforting tingle: he was flying, as carefree as he had been on Alderon an epoch ago.

"Remain stouthearted," he advised. "Shirk not the resolve of your forebears, nor worry much of the dark arts. Fortify yourself with all faiths and claim perseverance as your chief virtue. Do not babble. Practice not the disciplines of demolishment and such. You are matter. It must be saved."

Now he could hear Putt Fenno. "Aarrgghh," he was groaning. "Ooommpphh." He looked like he'd just lost his hands.

"Bear with me, my audience of earthlings," Bobby said, the weapon spilling from his hand. He had only a little more to say, specifically facts about souls and assurances of the next worlds, then this business would be finished; and soon— no more than a delfine, certainly—he would be home again, in that land of his infancy, that place of twelve red skies and crooked, hearty trees of gold.

BE FREE, DIE YOUNG

Down here in New Mexico, death isn't the special thing it is to you outlanders. My wife, Darlene (who has a Master's Degree, is a reader and knows about such), says that the dark thing we're taught to dread is no more unusual to us and our deserts than wind which blows ardently or noise from an unexpected quarter. Out here, we die by wreck or in a tide of shed domestic bloods. We're a shooting people, we are, driven to temper by the common rages: envy, sloth in the one we adore, covetousness. Once, for example, five years ago, I was in the El Corral, a bar in which gloom predominates, and heard a woman addressed in the following fashion: "Honey, I like that flesh which rises to meet the meat which seeks it." He was a Rotarian named Krebs and did believe, evidently, in speech of the oracular kind. There was silence, followed by a commotion with the murder-filled head and he-man arms of a boyfriend and then, such as I see it, the usual end, meaning spilled fluids and the gray, loose flesh of that which, in another time and place, might say, "My-my, what a tender hold we have on life." Yes, I have seen these citizens of America shotgunned, clubbed with a two-by-four, clobbered by a Chevy pickup and dragged up into a twisted repose on a ditch bank, and so I do not bring to our story of struggle and demise much sentiment or the weep-stuff you find in picture shows.

Listen: I wasn't always the hard nut I am now. To be true, I was that youth you sometimes see in old drunks—mournful and misty-eyed and easily swept into melodrama. I had a dog once, Raleigh, that stumbled into my room one day, slack-lipped and not tidy as I knew him. "What's wrong with you, boy?" I said. His head cocked, I saw a yellow tooth or two, and then he pitched over like a log. Mother says I made these noises: 'Aaarrrggghhh" and "Oooowwww" and would not accept for comfort any Bible-inspired language about mortals and the happy, fatted flocks that all animals gather into in the Protestant hereafter.

Which was pretty much my reaction—and why I'm telling you this—when, before I married her, Darlene's father, Dub Spedding, pointed a shiny lady's pistol at me, eyed me into silence and vowed to blast me over the raging waters of limbo and into hell itself if I ever bothered his child again.

This was 1968, you understand, a time of agitation I had sympathy with. To be honest, I was what my fifth-grade youngster Buddy calls a *hooper*, which is, as picture books define it, a middle-class creature with the hair and grave aspect of a bohemian; I had the slump of a revolutionary and went about, in these arid lands, as a teenage philospher in Beatle boots. I said things like "Be free, die young" and

"Fact and fantasy are never twice the same." In the rock-'n'-roll band for which I was the drummer, Wet Places at Noon, I sang of wrath and tranquil islands in the outer worlds, then made flirtatious eye contact with the thirteen-year-old nymphets who worshipped us. I smoked red-dirt marijuana, ingested Black Beauties and sometimes, thrown into the underhalf of my character (that half of Vandals and Visigoths, in which we all share an interest), I broke into establishments like the Elks Club and did, to use the lingo we spoke in those days, co-opt the pinball machines.

I was in love, of course; and on this day I am talking about I appeared at Darlene's house in my usual costume of fringes and convict leathers. We were to shop, I believe, during which I could do something to express my outrage against the bourgeois principles of order and money.

"I can't," she said. "Daddy says I got to stay here. We're having company.

It was noon and I was standing so that I could see nothing but sunlight and dark shape. This was, as is said in storybooks everywhere, foreshadowing.

"How long?" I said.

She told me to go home, she'd call. "He's real mad at you, Dwight. I think you'd better stay away for a while."

At home I snarled at the TV, then invented a song about pageantry and gore. I was profound in those days and liked to turn my vast valedictorian's intelligence upon what Mrs. Levisay used to call those existential questions—notions about identity and being which always made the FFA students and Vo-Ed folks sleepy as cats. In these times, I tell you, I was interested in what made this planet spin, why the upside seemed so often down and how the brain of Mr. Nixon worked. Now, I think of naught but comforts and how to preserve them.

By sundown, she hadn't called, so I tried her. There was, as you are right to expect, no answer.

"Okay," I said, "I'll nap."

I suspect now that my dreams were the vulgar male kind—wrought up with maidens and related froth; but, as I am now in a romantic habit of mind, let me believe that, at the so-called unconscious level, I knew something was wrong. My dreams, I therefore wish to believe, were turbulent as dark waters, heavy with peril, and omen-filled as are all moments before disaster.

It was the next day, Saturday, when I got up. No answer.

I told my daddy I was going over to Darlene's.

"The hell you are." He was a paving contractor, plus a County Commissioner, and had a direct way of speaking his piece. There was some work to do around here, he said. Specifically a willow tree to be ravaged and some compost to tote.

"Then I can go?"

He spit, looked into heaven. "We'll see."

That morning, well-baked by the sunshine we're famous for, I had these questions: What is going on? Where is that girl? We'd been going together for almost four years, and the assumption was that we'd be married one day. I was just in my settling-out period, I'd say, growing into the wise figure who could shoulder all those burdens parents hereabouts threaten their offspring with.

"Okay," Daddy said after noon, "you can go now. You be back at five. We're eating out, at the Popp's."

Lickety-split, I was there. Her place was deserted. I looked in the corral out back where Dub kept his horses, Bo and Skeeter. I rang the doorbell a thousand times. I sat by the pool for about an hour. I counted bricks. I even called the funeral home.

"This is Dwight Eugene Winger," I said, employing the polite voice my mother still loves so much. "And I'd like to speak with somebody from the Spedding family, please."

Dub's a mortician and, in keeping with the theme I am developing herein, well acquainted with death. He doesn't think much of it either—just sees us humans as bulk with several holes to plug. For him, death's the fact which feeds his family and makes him, of the six thousand folks here in Deming town, rich beyond want and able to laugh at this vale others find so tearful.

"Dwight Winger, is that really you?"

I was talking to George Dalrymple; in our high school, he was a dufus.

"Where are they, George? I got to speak to Darlene."

"I ain't supposed to tell," he said. "Dub says you're an old shithead and we're glad."

He was speaking for those other dipsticks who worked for Dub. They had their eyes on Darlene and saw me—in the context of the old story this is—as a Martian, clearly unfit for the darling who was the boss's daughter.

"I could beat the shit out of you," I said. "How 'bout I come down there and rip your heart out."

You could hear sputtering from that coward.

"There are three of us," he said. "Why don't you find a hole and crawl in it?"

All afternoon, I sat outside Darlene's place. I was in the grip of self-doubt, indeed. I had the sweats and such frets as

arise when event exceeds expectation; I imagined, I now
recall and feel no shame in admitting, that my thoughts were
like downed power cables, snapping and whipping and spitting sparks. Later, I called everywhere—the house they had
in the mountains that they went skiing on, Darlene's granny
in Roswell, friends from her Theta Chi days, that meager
marina at Elephant Butte where they took the boat sometimes. I was having, I realize, my moment: the crossroads
of time and circumstance in which it is revealed to you, as
truth is revealed to those bosomy heroines my momma is
always reading about, just what you want and are henceforth
meant to have in this world. I wanted Darlene; and I knew
it just as I know now that I am thirty-six, a graduate of Texas
A&M, and the sort of moral being who appreciates golf,
drink, and the regular embrace of a wife.

After dinner at the Popp's (it was spaghetti and whole-
some conversation), I got an answer at Darlene's It was
Marva, her sister, herself a knockout and dream-worthy.

"Slow down, Dwight. What're you talking about?"

Evidently, I was incoherent; it would be reported later that
I sounded Arab or Etruscan and did use the language of
madness and murder.

"You just tell me where she is," I said, "and I'll be gone."

"Daddy says we mustn't talk to you," she said. "He says
you're a drug-smoking, cheating asshole."

There was some talk, she said, that I'd stolen an Oldsmobile and that I'd taken it, plus a sixteen-year-old blonde
Wildcat cheerleader, into the mesa to do another thing the
law would love to know about.

That wasn't me, I said. It was just fellows I played music
with—Poot Taylor and fat Chuck Gribble.

"Daddy says you're taking money from a woman named Eve."

Then I felt it: "Darlene's with somebody, isn't she?"

"Daddy says you have no character at all, no ambition, no nothing. You're just using his little girl."

"Well, I'll be dipped," I said. I'd felt insight reach me like a fist in the ear. "It's that Frank Papen, right?"

"What Darlene needs, Daddy says, is a gentleman, not a punk who talks fast."

Frank Papen. He was one of those straight-shooting suitors who liked to hang around Dub, pretending to be interested in something more than his own daddy's bank. You can still see him nowadays, driving around in his Monte Carlo, wearing a flattop, and affecting the manner of one who is brisk in the business of mortgages and capital. His wife, I am told, is somewhat of a tragedy herself and keeps him otherwise busy looking up words like "solicitous" and the German for "despair."

"What would happen," I asked Marva, "if I came over there right now?"

Nothing, she said.

"Because they're off hiding someplace, right?"

I was smart, she said. Surely smart enough to see that my ways needed changing.

"Like what?" I said.

Like not be such a smarty-pants, she said. And maybe love America more.

"Marva Louise Spedding," I said, "you tell Darlene that I will be over at your place at ten o'clock tomorrow night. You tell her that I love her and that Frank Papen is to her what shit is to Shinola. You got that?"

"Make it later," she told me. "You're not supposed to know they're in Albuquerque.

That night, my band had a DeMolay dance to play and I attacked those drums as I had read that Batygh the Tartar had slain his enemies. The place was as you are probably picturing it: smoky as Dante's underworld, littered and full of din. We played my song, "Woman at Her Window," and made it speak for the many, like me, who were hungry but could not eat (which is metaphor and part of what I'm proud of). I was as apart from myself then as I am now from the boy who is the hero of this tale. I didn't drink, nor try a little of Poot's Mexican weed. Even Chuck Gribble's girlfriend could not tempt me.

She was wearing the outfit of an Egyptian and shimmied over to seduce me with her midriff.

"Mary Jane," I said, "I know someone that makes you look like the viper you are."

For dreams that night, I had none—not turmoil, not thrash, not mumbo-jumbo you get from Doctor Jung. I slept undisturbed, like a rock or a far-off fleecy cloud. Indeed, as I have since described it to Darlene, my sleep was that which does belong to, say, Clint Eastwood or those other righteous cowboys whose troubles are swiftly resolved by daring deed or single word.

In the morning, I was up early and went directly to my daddy.

"What needs doing?" I said. "I've been fooling around too long."

He looked around several times to see where my voice was coming from.

"You stay put, relax," I said, "I'll do the work today."

The way I figured it, even if they left now—Dub, Darlene, fawning Frank Papen, Dub's new wife Sylvia—it would take them nearly seven hours to get home. It was time, I believed, I could put to fine use by digging up Mother's flower beds or mowing the front yard. Plus, I sought to occupy my mind, turning its powers to such issues as which was weed, which not. Around noon, I had another idea.

"Ray Berger," I said, when I got him on the phone, "how much you charge for a haircut?"

It was Sunday, he said. I could come in on a weekday like everybody else.

I looked into my wallet. "I'll give you thirty-five dollars."

He spent a moment hemming, perhaps scratching his ear.

"I'll wash your car," I said, "pick up around your place, too."

By evening I had the hairdo you see everywhere in these times—lots of ear and neck, and impervious to breeze.

At home, I threw on a loud sportcoat Mother had spent a fortune on at the White House in El Paso. "Holy moly," I said. In the mirror was the person I hadn't been for five years. Had you seen him, you would have said that here walks a young man who has an upright God and keeps his face turned toward the lighter, higher airs goodness breathes in.

Then I waited.

As a man and a father and a taxpayer, I know many things now, for experience is a masterful teacher. I know, for example, the danger of impatience and why bullies are as they are. I know, furthermore, that we gringos are just one of many terrible, inward tribes. I know that TV corrupts and that there's more pleasure to be had in Barbar and Charles Dickens than in the thousand laugh-filled hours after the TV news. I know we can be cross one minute, humble the next and, in the third, touched by such everydayness as sunsets and certain music. But I do not know now, as I did not then, how to wait.

"Ninety-nine bottles of beer on the wall," I sang, cheerlessly, "ninety-nine bottles of beer ... "

Around ten the phone rang and I grabbed it up as if it were treasure. It was Marva.

"Darlene will be on the front lawn by the pool in exactly a half-hour," she said.

She had chosen to whisper, and I felt caught up in true mystery. This was an instant as rich as any from *Ivanhoe*.

"One day," I said, "when I am your brother-in-law, you will be able to ask me for anything."

Death. Say the word a dozen times and you'll see that it will mean as little to you as gibberish in French or what machines speak. Sung as we used to sing about what we thought was love in those days, it will no more touch you than trouble among South Pole penguins or quarrel across town; it will seem to you now as it seemed to me then—a condition fetched up to disturb the small minds we celebrate.

This is how it was:

I beat Darlene to the meeting spot on the lawn and she approached like abracadabra made of chiffon and dew. She was wearing a nightie, and in the almost complete darkness she looked white as a ghost. She had the dreamy movements of one who has slept for two centuries. (On our honeymoon a year later, up in Hot Springs, she told me that Sylvia had given her Valium and something watery to ease her thoughts.)

"What's going on?" I said. "I heard you were with a peckerwood."

She had the fluttery presence of a matinee female, and in
that moment I felt something dry and small break free inside
me.

"I believe we're over, Dwight. They talked to me for two
whole days, and what I know about you is scandalous."

She had a list, she told me, which included petty theft,
disrespect and my supposed allegiance to chaos.

I said, "Look at me."

I drew myself up stiff as pride.

I said, "I am complex, Darlene." I believe I mentioned
growth and described myself as but one point on the arc that
was all youth. I mentioned, as well, that I had virtue—
brought out now by trial and this tribulation; that, until this
minute, I had been ignorant of my true needs. I loved her,
I said. Were love electricity, then I had enough for a small
country.

"Daddy doesn't care," she said, "he's coming out here to
shoot you."

Dub Spedding had guns everywhere—in his nightstand,
under the front seat of his Eldorado, in each of his funeral
cars, plus a rack of exotic weaponry in his den. He had shot
deer and duck, and once he'd winged a Juarez wetback who'd
tried to bust in the back door.

So, in the cause-and-effect world we're looking at here, it
was at this instant that Mr. Spedding came thumping out his
front door, pistol in hand.

"Eeeeffff," I groaned. "Ooooowwwww."

You should have seen him in those days: three hundred
pounds of hard meat, on top of which sat a mind that won-

dered of little more than ends and the means to them. "Robust" is a good word. As are "dark-browed" and "violent."

"Darlene," he roared, "get inside."

Holding her hand, I could smell myself: part English Leather, part ooze the fear glands sweat out.

"I told you, Dwight." Darlene was crying, her hands flapping madly—to her hips, to her eyes, in the air like birds.

This was my thought, exactly: Dwight, this man is capable of eating you alive.

There was nothing for a second, then Darlene went flying from me as if snatched up by an angel.

I saw a light flash on in the Tipton house down the way and wished for an instant that I was near it.

"Daddy," she was saying, "I just hate you for this. I think he truly loves me."

Then she was stumbling backwards, spinning and holding herself where her own bullet might go.

"Boy," Dub Spedding said to me, "stop that damn shaking."

He came at me slowly. Lumbering. A thing familiar with disrepair and human havoc.

"Howdy, Mr. Spedding," I said. "How're you tonight?"

He fixed that gleaming silver pistol against my chin and I could feel an organ kicking inside. His face brought to mind the words *pitch* and *sulphur,* and he looked at me as others look at leaf rot or wastepaper. I was just an inconvenience he'd have to scrub off the porch one day.

"I know the sheriff," he began, "several folks in the FBI, even the Captain of the State Police. Your death will only be a remarkable accident to them."

We are one thing in this life, I was thinking. And sometimes we are another.

So then, because this was a long time ago and your hero was a fool, I said, "Mr. Spedding, don't say no more, just go ahead and do it."

The first dead person I ever saw was a ten-year-old boy who had tried to dig himself a cave in the side of a dirt culvert up where the Interstate is now. I was riding motorcycles with a couple of friends, Jimmy Bullard and John Risner, and we reached the scene as those ambulance people were pulling him out of the collapse and trying to revive him. It was a peaceful scene, what it was, blue heavens and vivifying sunlight and at the center of it—if I may be poetic—flesh which once had a name and a place in time. I remembered being struck by how composed that boy seemed. Though sallow-faced and blue at the lips, he seemed a charmed thing to me. He was not sex, which I knew a little of, nor the fame and riches we all wish for. He was not the world beyond, nor the future we boys sometimes talked about. He was, I know now, nothing—quiet, inert and eternal.

Which, I suppose, is what Dub Spedding saw in my eyes in this Wonderland I am writing about.

"Boy," he said, "what the hell are you thinking of?"

Darlene was elsewhere, sobbing and saying what a heartbreak she'd be to that father who'd killed her only lover.

He still had his tiny pistol at the point of my chin; you could tell he thought me as remarkable as a smart-talking Chinaman.

"I was thinking about the next world," I said. I mentioned that in it, as we were now, were me and him and her and it, his weapon.

You could see the air whoosh out of him then.

"Shit," he grumbled, dropping his arm and backing away.
"Go home, Dwight. We'll talk about this tomorrow."

I speak of the foregoing now because of what happened
this morning, and because I intend to leave you in a hopeful
humor. Dub and I, you should realize, are great pals now:
I am the perfect son-in-law and he, the perfect granddad,
generous with money and time. And this morning we were
out in the stable in the back, shoveling manure and, as he
says often, chewing the fat. He's old now, mildly diabetic,
and, as a retired person, he's given himself over to earnest-
ness. He likes to speculate on the drift of the world and its
current climate of decay. He likes to offer advice, particularly to the editors of *Newsweek* magazine. He sees them much
as he did see me once upon a time—as brainless and inconceivable as talking carp.

In any case, what he said, while we drank Coors beer and
shoveled, was this: "Dwight, how you think you're gonna
die?"

It was early and you could hear the gay splash-noises of
my children and Darlene in the pool in front of the house.
This was our fifteenth wedding anniversary and we'd come
over to frolic.

"Me," he was saying, "I'll probably go in a hunting accident or maybe a new wife will do me in." He was leaning on
his shovel, in his eyes those lights you might find in, say, Old
King Cole. "What about you?"

I knew of course. But didn't tell him.

What I didn't say was this: I am already dead. In a way,
I died the night he put the gun to my head and showed me
what a splatter I'd make on his pajamas; and the fact of

it—like the facts of all these many and cheap deaths in the contemporary world—means as little to me now as does the former unhappy self I was.

"Dub," I said, "let's go have us a swim, okay?"

Whereupon I put down my spade and made for the front of the house to see that which I had and the place we are here for.

THE ELDEST OF THINGS

Mozer's first dealer was a Latino named Spoon who roared up Chester out of Hough each Thursday in a vintage black-over-white Mercury so sweetly tuned it seemed capable of speech—a thunder as throaty and pure, Spoon told him once, as oratory itself. Spoon would park behind the Church of the Covenant, and Mozer would appear a little after noon, just before his class in the Romantics. The method was always the same: Spoon would say "Man!" and "Madre!" and "Don't be sneaking up like that, hombre!" and Mozer would slip himself into that auto slowly and with great ceremony, its interiors so full of red plush and shiny leathers it could have been the giant steel shoe of Satan himself. Spoon always had the radio tuned to JMO, or another spade station, his head, with its fertile hairdo, bobbing to a rhythm Spoon identified as equal parts funk and blood-stuff, the bass in the door speakers so heavy it seemed to pound on

Mozer's leg, maybe make a bruise, leave a welt. Spoon always dealt primo toot, iced and crystal, white enough to be a starlet's thigh, which he presented to Mozer in a glassine packet, rolling his Juarez eyeballs heavenward, saying the blow in question was either Chilean or direct from the Golden Triangle, strong enough to bend iron or set off train noises in the deep, primitive corners of your brain pan. Mozer always did a sample, which was protocol, the first snort bitter and laden enough to send him in search of words like *churl* and *hunch*. Then he paid, in old bills, Spoon the superstitious sort who thought of new money the way the Huns thought of achievement in bronze. They'd say adios, Spoon still caught up in the throes of thump and new music.

"You be careful," Spoon would say. "Maybe one day you don't want no more nose, okay? Maybe you go loco, want to be a bird or flashy gangster."

The female came into Mozer's life during that one semester he was calling Coleridge and Keats "tangents of lust" and "the milk-spurned bards of indecent closure," a pair like Mutt and Jeff, one full of limp and midnight oil, the other a dingus on the up-side of the perilous peak that was a wintry but heartening time of versifiers. It was the coke, he figured, that made him blabber that way: the several lines before class each Tuesday and Thursday that spun him into the lecture hall in a state he accepted as wired and supreme, all about him afflicted and cast low. Exercises in wonder, his lessons were breathless accounts of perfection and the mysteries which attend knowledge, which invariably ended with him throwing off his sportcoat, or climbing onto his chair, and shaking his fists as if he were leaving this life for fable and legend.

Elaine Winston was a Miltonist, a first-year Assistant Professor with an office on the first floor, and, as he learned happily, herself mad with learning. His hair slicked back, he went to her one day, followed her into her office after seeing in her face what he was convined was scepter-love and, well, theophany. "Miss Winston," he said, his voice full of his Louisiana upbringing, "lookee here." Yet, before she could sit, even before she could say "Hello," Mozer placed on her desk a vial of fluff Spoon said could launch you into Deityville by way of your own biles and ferments. It was Colombian rock, Spoon had said, mayhap as old as the earth itself, on account of it had evil in it, which led to an expanded view of the universe, which led in ultimate terms to a consideration of shit like Hierarchy and Ultimacy itself. Mondo heavy stuff. Made you wanna bark, perform a foulness with your fingers. Took the contemplation right out of daily business of finding and keeping.

Both of them agreed later that it was no surprise that immediately, her hands steady with purpose, she opened the vial and, with the patience of a DEA assassin, laid out two thin but exact lines. After all, she told Mozer, she'd read the literature and had been to the movies; plus she'd watched TV and, in her UC–Santa Barbara days, had tried root and downers and something which a now-lost boyfriend had described as Laotian, a melted fungus which you waved before your lips and lugged with you into Old Night—which was what Mozer yearned to hear; so, as he locked the door and switched off the light and unzipped her teacher's skirt, he was saying the Lady—the toot, the snow—was, like themselves, the outmost work of Nature, much beyond havoc and spoil and that they, Elaine Winston and himself, Richard E. Mozer (of Tulane and the University of Texas–Austin), would soon be passing beyond tumult and din for the uplifting horizons of organized beauties and that composite body in which incorruptible matter predominates, love.

For months after this, through a Cleveland winter frigid and piled with ice and into a glorious spring, Mozer's lectures were magic and biology both—hour-long sessions even the student newspaper, *The Observer,* in an unsigned editorial, called bifurcated and multifarious, "the eldest of things." One period Dr. Mozer spent on Shelley's "Music, When Soft Voices Die," spotting in its eight lines neither the beloved nor the quick, but privation and deficiency—in his mind the vision of a serpent with hips leading a legion of duteous and knee-crooking knaves. When he grabbed the chalk and dashed to the board to scrawl figures of analysis, he looked like a caveman, his face beleaguered, as if he'd embraced all his rascally needs. He told Elaine Winston, and she him, that they were entering a time of gulf and effulgence and pouring forth—a time washed by the waters of Abana and Pharpar, a time of fawn, renegado and hapless wight! During another class period, when he was to be addressing the horned moon and Mr. E. K. Chamber's *A Sheaf of Studies,* he fixed his head against the bosom of Mindy Griffith, a South Philadelphia sophomore COSI major, and claimed to hear, through her sweater and blouse and brassiere, not the heart but the steady, fairyland tromp-tromp of Mister Wordsworth's footsteps in the Rydale woods. "No bramble," he whispered. "No evergreen, no palm." Then, holding her by the shoulders, he said there was in her courage and outlawry, even the wonted face renewed.

That March, when he should have been concerned that

Elaine Winston was speaking of warmth and beach fronts and sweat, he began telling his classes about his family, offering his vision of child-rearing and where woe comes from. And one day, after taking a richness from Spoon that was said to have come from the very ash, honest, of the rood itself, he informed his class, while his organs beat like a Sousa drum corps, that he'd had no youth at all, that he had vaulted across the decades, from gamete to scholar, without benefit of the swerve and downwardness of adolescence; and that, were he to wed, it would be to a woman whose face had something in it of friskiness and of thorn.

That afternoon, drinking Pepsi under a young maple in front of Gund Hall, Mozer told Elaine Winston of the goody Spoon had promised him: a mixture likened to the tears of a lost people—the Goths, say—cocaine cut with the subsoil those NASA technicians at Lewis Research Center were bringing back from Uranus, stuff that made fire of water, earth of air. Lord, he said, it was itself love. Which was the gift, he told Professor Winston, he most wanted to give her, conveying this wish by licking her hands and mentioning conglobed atoms and seminal forms and female divinity. "No," she said. "I can't." He imagined them on the flaming ramparts of the world, him crafty and gaunt, her light incarnate. "I'm sorry," she said. "It's impossible." He mentioned glimmer, heart-baking rays, splendor. "Please," she sobbed, "no more." It was love, he said, and were she coke, he would now be at her toes, she that blessed white rail that stretched to infinity, she that orbit of song and purity; he was ready, he insisted, for bliss.

It was then, while he kissed her cheeks and eyes and forehead, that she confessed she'd taken another job. In Florida. She would be leaving at the end of the term.

■

For his next appointment, Mozer went flying toward Spoon's Mercury like a hawk with serpent wings, his topcoat flapping, his ski cap pulled shut over his ears. He believed that his innards, all link and hook and snap of them, were frozen, rattling like bolts in a bucket. He was sobbing, too, and even before he flung himself into the car, he was well into the latest chapter of his life, that unlightsome and diminished part, that part of yoke and aery gloom. Mozer saw himself in the upper waters of this world, drowning. He gagged and felt something inside—his spleen, he thought, or junked heart!—bang free. While Spoon studied him, Mozer spoke of the circumfluous liquids, calm upon which the World is built, the metaphorical jasper, the unmixed fire, the goo and slop, the *pneuma* of the Stoics. He told Spoon about Elaine Winston's decision and the wreck he was because of it; and, watching students gingerly tread the ice-slickened sidewalks near the building next to him, he speculated on the nature of man, the hylomorphic principle, multiple and gross, of substantial composition into the material world. He spoke of the *Fons Vitae* of Avencebrol. The *Hokmah*. The *Yod* and the mysterious *AWIR*. He said, before running out of breath, that he was dumped, mashed, crazed, wrung out, wracked, and no more good for this world than war.

For a second, while those on Spoon's radio sang to them of high-heeled sneakers and wig hats, neither spoke. Then, like a hungry man sitting down to a thirty-dollar T-bone, Spoon said, "Doc, don't worry. I have just the thing." And from nowhere—or the next world, Mozer thought later, or the world after that—appeared several grams of doody cut fine as morning mist. It was a weight, Spoon assured him as he left the car, that in minutes would strip away the pain and lay bare the shiny, cartilaginous root of himself, his spring and heavy, greased wheel.

During April, Mozer got used to the idea she was leaving by rededicating himself to his work. It was, he would say later, his period of plucking up and casting out, a time of victual and wound. He scratched out a paper on "So We'll Go No More A-Roving" for the MMLA section on Byron for the St. Louis meeting, a paper he delivered with such a sorcerer's fury that it appeared to many in the Marriott suite that, at a mention of laurel and myrtle, he might burst into flame. He mumbled about "features of intelligent genera" and marched into class wearing a rag around his ears, saying he was pity and Dido's pyre, that heavy-headed carouser who was the sin of apotheosis given tendon and hackle. In one class, rolling on a circuit made smooth and gleaming by two lines of what Spoon claimed was flake chipped from the planet's first tree, Dr. Mozer forged a lecture that linked, in a moment quiet enough to have come from death, the Ens, the hinder parts of God's essence and the "houmoousian," the latter of which his pupils were not to conceive of as the Father and Son and the Holy Ghost, but as Larry, Curly and Moe—the modern Wise Men of burlesque and pain. It was an insight, Mozer noticed, that left eager Mindy Griffith limp with hope.

The following Tuesday, in the parking lot of the Church of the Covenant, the sky dark with soot, Mozer told Spoon he wanted stuff that said smote and wither, that would his soul and bounteous fortune consecrate. "An ounce," he said; Spoon, in a yellow fedora that could have come from a Mickey Spillane book, nodded gravely. "You feeling low,

Doc?" he wondered. Mozer said that he and Elaine—for old time's sake, really, one final fling—were taking a room in the Shoreway Holiday Inn during finals. He used the words *mode* and *issue*. "I can dig it," Spoon said and in an instant, as if it had materialized from the black world, Spoon was placing on the seat between them a Baggie which contained a substance that, to Mozer's mind, seemed, apart from its glow and density, to be living. "No mas," Spoon was saying. "As of today, I am out of business." He was going back to Mexico, he allowed, where an acquaintance, a bighearted caballero like himself, was in league with an hombre who knew a figure who had contact with the so-called, which might develop, given ingenuity and gorge, into a future of *resplandor,* radiance. There was mucho dinero to be made, he added. A man in the grip of an idea, he said, could go anywhere in his life. Mozer felt the world tilt, the sky crumble into a hole at the horizon. "What about me?" he said. There was music in the car, of course, metals and whines. "I thought we had an understanding," he said. "Amigos." Spoon was making smacking noises; he said not to worry, the Professor was muy especial, he was being turned over to a gent—"like a colleague, man"—who, in Mozer's moment of need, would appear, bringing some Lady that was virtually coeternal with the Father Himself.

As he would reveal to his next dealer, The Suit, and the one to follow him, and the one to follow him, his week with Elaine Winston, now departed Assistant Professor, was lived in a place unapproached through necessity and chance. It was part manifestation, he said, part similitude. A haven hewn from hardiment and hazard. "There were no hard feelings," he would say, "no guilt." The first two days, they lived off room-service chicken and wine and that varlet's concoction which, Elaine swore, made you use the terms *hath* and *ye*. It turned thought to deed, and that to a thing which uttered. If anything, Mozer would declare for years, they both grew more luscious: She was the bringing forth and the shining unto; he, decree and ascent. He sprinkled lines on her breasts and thighs and once entered the whooshing, ornamented, fibrous, unnettled chambers of her heart, as she sang to him of the whip and the cradle, the prattling bush and the metabole. Later, he laid a trail which led over a dresser, across the floor, to a coffee table, climbed a chair, followed the curtain folds and ended, it seemed, at the mouth of a warm cave, the first principle of things—"the junction," he hollered, "of form and meaning!" In his joy, he became ape and first man, a being of lope and skinned knuckle and savage mien.

After the third day, and until they left for the airport, they didn't again use the phone or open the drapes. One time, after not speaking for an hour, he went to her as he imagined Keats had gone to his Grecian Urn, muttering of the dales of Arcady, plus pipes and timbrels. She was lamentation, he told her. He looked into her ear, discovering a spot to put everything: his smoking brainstem, the shame and prize of himself, that ragged wind in his chest. An hour later, he found himself yelling about the cataract and trodden weed. She—no, not she alone, but she who was Eve and Sweet Betsy from Pike and Mother Hubbard and Radio City Rockette—she was garland and seashore and silk. She was, he decided, swarm populous and writ itself—chaste, messy writ, like a message from the soul. "In me, there's the rose,"

Elaine Winston said. And ire. And compass. And kirtled Sovereign. Mozer, collapsed against the bathroom door, was applauding. He was seeing everything, from beginning to end—from bang in the dark, through swamp and savannah and bustling boulevard, to bang in the dark. And then she stood at the end of the bed, its sheets a snarl of white, her breasts heavy and dark, her head so far away it seemed she was scraping the ceiling. There was in her, she vowed, alimental recompense and humid exhalation. She was quoting, he knew. There was, she was saying, a progeny of light. And recess of miracle. And supernal expanse. And when she finally pitched back onto the bed, exhausted, she was talking about optic emanation and preparation and the all-embracing, without which there could never be any, yes, privilege.

In the next hour he knew, even without his watch, that it was time to go, that days five and six had passed. What had come to him, he decided, was understanding; and it came when, feeding from a line that seemed composed of socket and hook and perfect mortise, he looked up and saw that her flesh was gone and what remained—what he slurped and bit and sucked, and what shouted to him of void and fathom and nitre—was not Elaine Winston, Miltonist, but his own love, brawling damp and full of fear. He saw his love as gnash and twisted limb and lips of dew. He saw it as text and high estate and supped wonders—a clamor of sally and retreat: unsorted, turbid, clip-winged and no more noble than a donkey in ferkin and wig. He saw himself as Mongol, pounding across a cedarn cove—that land of S.T. Coleridge!—hot for the maid that was passion: a chase which would take, he realized, forever.

■

Mozer's second dealer, The Suit, was an insurance lawyer who toiled downtown and did not care, as Spoon had, about music or shiny vehicles. He was a Yale grad who, as promised, wanted to discuss life and the meaning thereof, who would arrange a meet in the men's room on the eighth floor of the Statler Office Tower on Euclid; and who would, before laying on Mozer crystal the size of a heavyweight's fist, address the context of coke, its bewitching history and its humble provenance. One time it was Mao-informed stuff, advanced but cryptic, scrutable only to those who knew of the universal hubbub and the mutiny of spirit. Another time the toot came from a slyboot, Lucretian kingdom and had to it much blindness and folly. On another occasion, the stuff was Hebrew, tartareous and cold.

Then there was the meeting before the start of the Fall term, when Elaine had been gone for almost three months. Quietly, The Suit locked the washroom door and plucked from his jacket pocket an envelope which held what The Suit said was sublimity itself, rumored to have come from the soaked deltas of Mars, misrule made elemental. "Jesus," The Suit said, placing the item on the counter. It appeared to be vibrating, as if it had breath and muscle. They peered at it awhile. Mozer said something about awe—the scalloped rim of the universe. The Suit nodded. Mozer said something about firmaments—the quaint auguries of nightswains. The Suit nodded. Mozer said something about glories, and when The Suit wondered what the Professor was going to do with this modern miracle, a light flickered on in Mozer's memory. He felt his brain shiver and quake, its meat darkening.

He had one idea, then a second—both electric and comely, as if he were a mathematician, a man versed in the joys of problem and its solution. There was, it seemed, a machine's click in his forehead, and he saw, The Suit still at his elbow, the crooked and croupy in himself limp away into blackness. He took a deep breath—the first in months, he believed— and he heard, as if with a castaway's ears, a shout and a call, human noise after eons of silence.

He was thinking about Mindy Griffith, that sophomore from Philadelphia, that one whose major in Communications Science had taught her, doubtlessly, the subtle and potent differences between talk and speech; yes, that fetching, unsafe creature who'd nearly left her desk that noontime when he'd read from the *Biographia* of shag and rack and dim, wicked hunter. Oh, he knew what he would do, all right. And he knew, too, that while one might say he'd have to be a pretty slimy motherfuck, at thirty-five, to hustle the innocent, another might say he'd have to be one hell of a fine person, confident as a gambler, with the guts of a Columbus, to share, to shepherd someone into that new world of love— that enchanted province of paradise and dread.

MARTIANS

Several years ago, about the time my wife Vicki began talking about suing me for divorce, my best friend, Newt Grider— who had to him all the virtues you expect from men in middle age—told me he believed in UFOs. We were on the sixth green of the Deming Country Club, only half-serious about our two-dollar nassau but thirsty as Arabs for the beers we would get at the turn, and for an instant, because he had the tendency to mumble or clown, I thought he was speaking French or trying out on me that Howdy-Doody double-talk he used to invent for the entertainment of his daughters.

"Boy, you don't believe in nothing," I said; it was banter, like that between Butch and Sundance. He had just smacked a driver and was watching his ball soar off into one of those sunsets our New Mexico has a reputation for, extreme and scary to the animal in us.

"Lamar Hoyt," he was saying, "I have known you a long time, right?"

We had been pals of the lifelong sort, since teenagers when we had been in the same Wildcat backfield. We had done everything together: lost our cherries to the same Juarez whore, took in the same experiences I hear described as necessary but usual. We even lived, in the time I am writing about, on the same block and had the same thoughts about what Vicki used to call the great themes of our age—how to vote, where love comes from and what to do with the weaknesses in you.

For a second—as long, I suspect, as it took for his ball to land in the way-off fairway—he just looked at me, eyes bright as new pennies, then he said that last night, while all of Deming town was asleep or rolled up next to its TVs, he was in his backyard, wearing only pajama bottoms and being addressed by beings from outer goddamn space.

"Shit," I said, "what're you talking about?" I was looking around for the joke, the way you do on April 1st when your children tell you the car's on fire.

"I'm serious," he said.

He had the same bent-forward posture he'd get when we played cards and a full house would suddenly appear in his hands—earnest as a Baptist, humor a thing for lesser souls who believed in luck.

"What do they look like?" I wondered. I was, of course, imagining the common alien: green, perhaps slime-dipped, plus the large, lopsided brain of a genius.

"They're luminous," he said, "like angels." They were about the size of my oldest boy Taylor, he said, which meant they resembled fifth-graders, and they traveled from what you now know is the Vega galaxy, a swirl of planets and dust older than time itself, and they were coming here just as they had been coming all along over the centuries, in magnificent vehicles which made our efforts at combustion and Top Secret propulsion look feeble as campfires. "You believe me, don't you?" he said.

His voice was dreamy as sleep and, yes, because he was my best friend, I was believing him, just as I have learned to believe, for example, those born-again folks who say that in their swimming pool one afternoon or sitting behind a desk at the Farmers and Merchants Bank there was first a thunderous crack, then something like firmament opening, and finally Christ Himself beckoning forth, all the choirs of the afterworld singing about love and wooden arks.

"You ever lose anything, Lamar?"

You should know that we weren't playing golf any longer; in fact, we were just standing to one side of the fairway, letting Mrs. Hal Thibodeaux and three of her lady friends play through.

Well, I told him, I'd lost a wallet one time and my high-school graduation ring and the keys to the Monte Carlo disappeared at least once a week.

"That's not what I'm thinking about," he said.

He was thinking about, specifically, people and objects, all those things which were said to vanish in spooky places—boats and planes, and all the people aboard them—plus citizens who were supposed to go to the movies or shopping at the Piggly Wiggly, or big animals, like cows and horses, which are one day there but gone the next. "They got 'em," he said. We were being probed, he told me, and mentioned many names from history of those who knew: a whiskered lunatic named Trismegistus, plus a tribe of fifth-century Hebrews, as well as most deep-thinking Orientals of modern times.

"How do you know all this?" I wondered.

They had told him, his small visitors. He had stood in his backyard, watched in breathless suspense as this vehicle had landed silent as snow, and they had popped out of something you would call a port and went up to him without the inconvenience of walking and put in his mind, instantly as magic, everything which could be read or spoken or thought. "You know what's up there now?" He was pointing at his own temples and eyeing me as if from a hundred miles away.

Near us, in an outfit most folks only wear on Sundays, Mrs. Thibodeaux was flailing with her five iron; and for a time, I confess, I wished I was part of her foursome talking about bridge or what to do with Green Stamps.

"Up here," Newt was saying, "is stuff about Lemnos and animus and quote the blood-dimmed tide unquote."

He was scaring me, he was, as he had frightened me months before when, soaked with Oso Negro and overtired, he'd shouted that what this republic needed was a good shit-storm, one which would bury the lot of us—him and me, too!—and thus teach us a thing or three about the small, damp beginnings of everything.

"What's Alice Mary say?" I asked. She was his wife and, from my view, sweet as any man deserved.

"She thinks like you do, that I'm loco." He was fingering his headbones again and making up such language, he said, as is exchanged between galaxies and the stark reaches of far-off orbs, utterances you can hear anytime from pigs or barnyard fowl. "They want me," he said, "and I do want them."

His plan, I learned, was to be swept up this very evening. "I'm going out in my backyard," he said, "look for them in twilight and go up when they say to." In his face was that divine look which, I suppose, has come over mystics in every age: bright flesh and eyes watery with bliss.

"What about the girls?" I said. I was trying to turn his mind to the practical. This was merely upset, I told myself. He was only angry, as we all get, or fretful about money matters.

"Lamar," he said, "come over here." He was like me in every respect, so I did as told. He threw his arms around me in that male way, part grapple and part clasp. "These people are my destiny, Lamar. They've known me before I was born, goddammit."

All the way back to the clubhouse, one arm still hung over my shoulder, he told me what a delightful world awaited him—air and rare mists and peace—all those words that sound great when you're drunk but in the full light of day, especially in the shitkicker paradise of our desert, sound sentimental as baby talk. "I'm going to be moving in another dimension," he said when we reached his pickup. He was still wearing his spikes, plus those shiny green slacks which always brought to mind Pinky Lee. "Say bye-bye to me, Lamar." He was shaking my hand, vigorously, and if I was thinking, I was doing so as more jelly than vertebrate, looking at him as if he was a fresh work of creation, something as shocking as another sun. And then, after he opened his door, he did a brave thing, which was to kiss me on the cheek.

"I'll miss you, Lamar," he said, "but I'll be keeping an eye on you from where I am."

This next part is the hard stuff, for I ask you to join me in forgetting for a moment that this is 1984 and that we have been to space itself and do have the Air Force and thousands of Ph.D.'s to tell us otherwise. I want you to think as I have read that Indians and other ancient peoples do—which, as I understand it, is with their hearts and in the company of wise, grumpy sorts from icy underworlds. What you already suspect is indeed true: nearly a decade ago, as it has been reconstructed by our police, Newt Grider, smiling like a ninny and got up (Alice Mary says) in a costume which was mostly bed sheet, did wander through his TV room, say no, thanks to a macaroni-and-cheese casserole, and drift like an ardent juvenile into his backyard from which—in a second or an hour—after some mumbling about twinkles and the cosmic items we are, he utterly and instantly vanished. For several days, Alice Mary was in the panic this deserved. No, she told Sgt. Krebs, there had been no fight, at least not a big one; and no, there was no other woman or any some such, as who would desire something doomed to be a fatso like Jackie Gleason? If they wanted to know, she said, why didn't they talk to old Lamar Hoyt?

"I bet he knows where Newt is," she said, "he's a son of a bitch, too."

For a week, exactly as I'd heard it, I told what I knew. I repeated it for Krebs and to a detective (who sported the Fu Man Chu moustache State Farm men wear) and once to an FBI fellow who wondered how long I'd had my Chevrolet dealership and was it true I'd once been to SMU? One afternoon, I even gave it to a reporter from the *Headlight,* a lady with a lively haircut which would have looked sharp on the corpse of Elvis Presley. It was a "profile" article, she said, but when it appeared, the Newt I loved was nowhere in it. I read stuff we all knew but had forgotten about: his setting fire, as a teenager, to a cotton field behind the Triangle Drive-In; his opening an irrigation canal and flooding Mr. Bullard's lettuce field; his having a certain drinking problem after the infant death of his only son. There was talk, too, of out-of-body travel and the belief in astrology, plus how you could divine the future in special leg bones. All of which, wrote that lady writer I was liking less and less, sounded like a voodoo smokescreen for a man who, like thousands and thousands of others in America, was just a plain, matter-of-fact runaway, vamoosed to Peru or another romantic kingdom in search of his lost youth.

It was in here, you must know, that Vicki moved out, taking our sons with her, and time (of which I am partly concerned) became mixed and fluid and dreadful. One day, I am saying, she was here and merely wrought up with the usual strife and dissatisfactions; the next day, she was off in Las Cruces, sixty miles east, living with a club pro named Ivy Martin and telling my children, Buddy and Taylor, that I was beast and dimwit and absolutely without ambition. On another day, I was divorced and lighter the five thousand dollars it cost; and on still another, I say, a year had gone by and I was skinnier by many pounds and lonely as a castaway. It was March, windy but good for sleeping, then it was January, raw as any scrape you get; then it was March again, and I'd look up from my reading and see the walls move (as they do when, for forty-eight hours, you haven't talked to anything except your own stubbed toe). I'd phone my boys every Sunday and hear about their soccer and that soon Ivy was taking them to Ft. Worth to rub elbows with Lee Trevino and Hubie Green and that Mother, my Vicki, was working at Mode-O-Day and maybe looked a little like one of Charley's Angels, all blouse and fly-away hair.

Then one day I grew the beard my shop foreman Poot Tipton said I ought to and started to go out. The first time, I remember, I stood in front of the mirror for an hour perhaps, studying myself as I have seen others look at my automobiles they can't afford. I said to myself such hopeful phrases as "You look good, Lamar, you really do," and splashed myself with a modern fragrance Buddy had sent for Xmas. I smelled like a jungle, I thought, which was maybe right for this world. Poot said I got lucky as that evening I met a woman at the Thunderbird (which is bowling alley and lounge, both); but she was herself divorced ("His name was Veloy and I hope he rots!") and ruined from it. At my house, she walked around and made faces at the knickknacks I hadn't thrown out. Her name was Merri Lu, I learned, but she was contemplating changing it in favor of one which complemented the exotic sense she now had of herself.

"How 'bout Reva?" she said. She was out by the pool, already unbuttoning her shirt. "C'mere, you bastard," she said, "call me Mia and you can have all of this."

At that moment, I took a look at myself and saw this: almost forty years old, a little bit Episcopalian, Libra to those who cared, modest about my money, and once upon a time a fair linkster.

"Miss Mia," I said, "why don't I take you on home?"

A month later I went out with Poot's sister, Randi. "You're looking studly, boss," he'd said, "you'd be doing her a favor." She had cheekbones I hadn't seen before, severe and red, and the posture of a hatrack. She smoked red-dirt marijuana and claimed she wanted me to join her in the hinterlands of spirit. "What're you thinking about?" she said. "I'm thinking about the Father of all Hindrance."

We were in the El Corral bar, a place of cowboy motif and welcome darkness, and I felt as apart from her as I had from Newt the day he disappeared. "You wanna hear about me," she said, "before we get back to your place?" From the bar across the way, I could hear two guys, both dressed like buckaroos, making liquor noises. I heard the word *woo,* I believe, and then a string of words, every other one of which was either Mex or obscene. "I look older than twenty-two, don't I?" Randi was speaking to me. "It's carriage and knowing your own mind." She had my chin in her fingers, my lips mashed together; and she had the eyes you see on starved Hindus in *National Geographic*—forty thousand years old and not tired. "I like you," she whispered, "you're gonna be good for my mind, I can tell."

Exactly here it was, in this story I am telling you, that I excused myself, said I had to go to the toilet, then left by the front door. I was heading, I think to that place I had been tending toward all along.

'Well, I'll be damned," Alice Mary said. "Look what's here on my doorstep."

In jeans and an old T-shirt that could have been Newt's, she appeared young; I was hoping she was still sweet, too.

"I like that beard," she said, "gives you an air."

In the light, she was touch-worthy and I had the urge, which I felt like a fist in the chest, to have her neck and bosom next to mine.

"Where are the girls?" I said.

They were at the Shelby's. A sleep-over.

I must've said a hundred things then, all forgettable and overused elsewhere, about what a tragedy our world was and what a peckerwood I'd become and how, when something broke, I didn't fix it; and then—bless her—she said, "You're letting the bugs in, close the door," and I followed her inside to a living room that had no trace at all of her absent husband Newt Grider. Something was swimming in me, stomach or neighbor organ.

"You'd like to have me, wouldn't you?"

What I said came out choked, but affirmative.

"You believe I'd like to have you too, don't you?"

That was true, also.

"It won't be any good, you know."

She was being tough, which this deserved, and I was grateful.

"I had a guy in here last week," she said. "Told me I was the saddest piece of ass he'd ever known."

I'd seen the truck. A Blazer, gray over white, one of its headlamps cockeyed. Plus a muffler my people could repair for under thirty dollars.

"Okay," she said, "let's try this thing."

Folks, there is something in a man, independent of his lustful underhalf, which loosens and grows light when a woman shows him that she's a creature too; time stops and even before clothes are shed, or noises made, there is something—composed of gland and the way you are taught, I suspect—that makes you think you are wise when you are dumb, able when you are not. Alice Mary was right: we were witless and fumble-fingered as virgins, shy and fearful. We tried for an hour, I think, even kissing a labor. As lovers are supposed to do, we went after each other in a fury, but, I am telling you now, all the heart was out of it. She was brave, and I was brave, and then, after it became certain that courage wasn't the substance called for, she said, "Lamar, I think you ought to go home now."

She had my underpants in her fist, being helpful.

"I could come over tomorrow," I said.

"No, you couldn't," she said.

She was right about this, too: there wasn't anything between us but her husband and my wife, and they were in the distant world.

"You're a cute guy," she said, "don't be a fool." She gripped me by the ears and kissed my nose, which is the feature most people see first.

And then, in what I know to be the end of this narrative, I was outside, my house down the street lit up like a ballpark. Its neighbors were all dark and middle-class, here and there a light bulb glowing. My heart felt as if it belonged to another man, leaky and floppy at the valves, and thoughts were reaching me as if by telegraph, clipped but steady.

"Okay, Newt Grider," I said, "where are you now?"

Everywhere the sky was random twinkle and black as the cape a witch wears. I was ready, I knew, as Newt had been—ready for our advanced visitors to hover near and draw your hero up into their world. I wanted to be where everything which is ever lost or put aside or misplaced is gathered together, waiting.

LOVE IS THE CROOKED THING

All of this happened years ago when I was the son-of-a-bitch I am not now.

I was Number 56 then, your gruesome Outside Linebacker; and, dressed up in my working-man's clothes of plastic thigh pad and Riddell headgear, I had this purpose on earth: to sunder (as in render) flesh and make it lie down quietly.

Which is how you become when you share your plot of turf with mud named Jitter and Dokie and The Prince of Fucking Darkness.

This is how I sounded then:

"Son," I would snarl at the tackle across from me, "do you know who I am?" And he, after swallowing hard the way the observant do when they recognize doom itching to mash them, would say, "Uh, of course," pent up with the fear I meant to put in him. Whereupon I'd turn to my compatriots and speak: "Did you boys hear what this pissant called me?"

They did, adding that such was not pretty nor fair-minded especially coming from, as the case might be, a TCU Horned Frog or Bear from Baylor. "Well," I would say, "don't come my way on account of this." Which was my massive arm and its inflexible cast, which might take the daylights and sense of him and put them in outer goddamn space.

More about me before we come to what I'm here about:

At my graduation, I moseyed across the platform in Razorback stadium and greeted the President in the customary manner, then surprised him by saying thus: "Archie, I'd like to speak a few words to these folks."

You could see he did not wish to quarrel with even one of the three hundred pounds I was. Plus, I was cum laude from this place, an expert among their groves of multiple choice and true-false.

"Burl Perteet," he said, "I would be honored," and he went wisely to his appointed chair.

I let the thousands gathered to watch bask in the shine of my smile.

"Citizens," I said, "you're looking at meat worth 400,000 dollars to the Lions of Detroit, ain't that grand?"

Picture the ooohh's and aaahhh's that followed.

"Here, look at this."

Whereupon Jitter and Dokie and several sophomores I'd browbeat conveyed my bedroom of trophies up here with me, the mass of which glimmered, as is said, unto such gold as is worshipped by minions everywhere. In addition, there was a sunshine that May afternoon worthy of Brother Homer and Wordsworth.

"These are what I got," I announced, "for being mean and excellent at it. Citizens, I can't imagine living another way, thank you."

Which brings us to the present moment, a dozen years from the above event, and how I come to be the charitable gent I am now.

In 1968, at the same instant your rookie Burl Perteet was called upon to sing his Alma Mater for all those veterans at training camp, a woman from the West Side of Cleveland, Inna Lee DuFoys, was learning that her husband, an E-4 named Coy in the employ of Uncle Sam, was dead many thousands of miles from her, slain by illiterate fourteen-year-olds in pajama-like outfits who did not, as we are wont to believe in these olden days, appreciate life in the precious sense those in America did.

At first there was no conflict: Coy came home in a box and was buried with a ceremony which included a flag and a chaplain's handshake, plus words aimed at healing over such scorched areas as those surrounding the heart and in the brain where memory lurks.

Then, about the time our hero Perteet was making his first start against the '49ers, Eddie Ivory, Coy's best pal, came back and said how it was over there—who was who, for instance, and what was what, and how to distinguish between them—telling enough so that Inna Lee could summon up a picture of her man among whirling rotors and the whomp-de-whomp of Incoming and the dozen colored smokes used to mark the LZs.

"Tell me more," she said, famished for details of this event which seemed so underhanded. "Well," Eddie said, "we went In-country R & R one time, at China Beach. I suppose you know about that." She did, to be true, but had to know more—about the warfood they ate, and what a piaster was, and how they slept standing up or in a squat; so, evening after evening, she learned about hardware which could melt a building, and the heart-stopping clank the wrong sound in the wrong place might make in those hearing it, and the spectacle of teenagers calling for intervention of the divine kind. "What were those sounds again?" she said. They were these: Splat and Aarrrggghhh and Boom-boom-boom.

And every night, after Eddie Ivory left, when she was some sore-hearted, she went deeper into the spot she was coming to know so well—a convergence of jungle and bug and random, hurly-burly violence. Some nights she could see Coy sprawled, all the limbs of him flung outward, his resting ground of leaf and soil as white and large as a Niagara Falls wedding bed. What's more, she even shared his thoughts—those of storm and flying metal and the calamity of phosphorus, thoughts that were four, then forty, then four million horrors at once.

She could see him walking, not at all the figure who'd married her in Cobb County, Georgia, and brought her to Cleveland so he could split steel at Republic and maybe make a little money. Skinny, looking made of bristle and spit, Coy was first in line, wearing a much-too-large helmet, his apparel scribbled over with words she didn't know he knew: *futile* and *fenestrate*. He had a calendar drawn in Magic-Marker on his fatigue shirt, all the June and July days X'ed out. He seemed awfully burdened, Coy did, what with flak jacket and well-oiled weapon and his face a mask of Avon horror-show, his features rubbed out in favor of the deep shadows common to this action he lived in. Inna Lee could plainly see his amigos and hear their brave chitchat and smell that Cambodian weed Coy said they smoked to keep their wits up. Always, she was in his blood, it seemed, when the turmoil commenced; and she felt, as he must've, his private alarms go off when the flora they hiked among burst into flame or became a hail that made an ooommmpphh noise piercing them. She heard him ask his leg for a thing it could not do; nor could his arm, it having been given a too-vicious wrench by something that sped past it buzzing like a wasp. She had his thoughts, too—those that were made into such speech as "Shit" and "My Lord!" and "Holy Mother!" And then—at the moment Burl Perteet was easing a Dallas Cowboy into never-fucking-never land—she was down and crawling, scurrying from shriek to howl and then stopping, knowing (with bleak amusement, even) that everything light and uplifting was being swamped by an onrushing dark tide which carried above it such trash as wife and home and living to an old age.

In 1974, Burl Perteet, twice an All-Pro, found himself in a court of law, his crime a prank the city couldn't accept the humor of. His was behavior, the *Free Press* wrote, such as required correction, on account of athletes being heroes to the young among us.

Yes, he and his roomie, Herkie Walls (Southern Mississippi, '71), had raided mostly white suburbs, stealing porch plants—in particular several poinsettias which belonged to the mayor of Grosse Pointe Woods.

"Aren't you ashamed of yourself?" the prosecutor wondered.

Burl turned his lavish smile upon those shopkeepers who were convicting him.

"You did see Mr. Walls take those decorations, didn't you?"

Our linebacker said he'd seen Mr. Walls do a hundred laugh-worthy deeds, but little with plant life.

"Like what?" that man said.

"Like dally with your wife, I believe."

That man rose up as if punched: "Your Honor!"

"You wanna hear the noise she uttered?"

That man got a hold of himself in a hurry: "Perteet, what kind of person are you?"

They were waiting, so he told them: "Mr. Prosecutor, I like to romp and care profoundly little about you and your ilk."

Which was how, in a week, he found himself the property of the Cleveland Browns. It was a trade designed to make everyone look smart, plus get a troublemaking mesomorph out of town; and Burl Perteet went hither as a man partial to jest and hurling his unwelcome bulk at the other guy's breastbones.

Six years later, one summer night, late, Inna Lee DuFoys woke up beside a man who was wearing a diamond earring shaped like the numbers 5 and 6 and who had such weight to him that, for an instant, the world seemed to tilt in his direction. It took her a minute to remember his name and that they'd left together after she got off work at the Crazy-horse, where she served drinks and sauntered about in a costume best described as skimpy. He'd said she had a body that those at *Time* magazine write about: all sinew, with the girth of Tinkerbell. Lord, he was a presence in that place, like clatter in a grave, those fellows with him given to whooping and slapping of the thick parts. He was a football player, he said, on that gridiron downtown where he did mayhem and got paid for it. Mostly, she remembered that being under him was like being buried in an avalanche which shook and spoke of itself as violence made living meat. "I like you plenty," he'd said. "Here, put up your fingers like this."

Now, up and about in this room, she wondered where she was. There was evidence of a wife perhaps, somebody whose pictures made her look punched and bruised, with hair upswept like a Roman helmet. Inna Lee's clothes were everywhere, as if stripped from her by a hurricane. This was a palace, she figured, big as a roller rink with everything in it—fuzzy carpet, furniture, even decorative doodad—courtesy of K-Mart. "What is that stuff?" she said once. "Tufts on suede is what."

She was half-dressed before she thought of the men she'd known since her time with Coy. There'd been that attorney who'd handled the GI insurance and other work she couldn't get the hang of. His name, she believed, was Tom and he liked to beat his chest afterwards and brag about the explosions in his head. That lasted a year. Then there was a period without companionship during which she worked as a teller at National City until Mr. Hensley made her feel like a hillbilly, which led to work at the Big O store on Chester Street. Then there came these fellows: Lamar Fike, and that Pepper Pike person named Schilling who drove the Mercedes, and two best friends named Gee Gee Gambill and "Hamburger James" (who said they worked for Elvis Presley once), and Hodge who used to take her to the Shoreway Holiday Inn, and that affair she got into with what's-his-name, the Astronomy professor at Reserve.

Then Eddie Ivory came back into her life. He'd been

working at the Twinsburg plant for Chrysler and said he hadn't done squat with his life except buy such vehicles as motorcycles and four-wheel-drive Broncos and drink to the point of forgetfulness. "I know what you want," she said; to her, life was as simple as grade-school arithmetic. "Okay," she said, "here." Whereupon her shirt came open and his face became like daylight again. Lord, this Ivory boy did weep a lot, even naked when such would seem impossible. He'd come to the door, at her Ohio City apartment, always with a bottle of George Dickel, his expression full of bad news and pity he hadn't earned. "Come in," she'd say, and in minutes they'd be at it, that embrace they were doing part wrestling, part hanging on. "What're your thoughts?" he said once. "I wasn't having any," she said, right away having plenty. Eddie was staring at the ceiling, specifically the water stain which resembled another man's angry face. Eddie was thinking about Coy, that time in March they were on loan to Hotel Company and visiting a pal of theirs, a mortar man with 1/26. "This guy was a killer," Eddie said. "He could be eating cheddar cheese and cling peaches and talking about greasing Charlie the whole while. You know what Coy said?" Inna Lee did not. "He said dying was shit to him. He said this was the United States Marine Corps we were talking about and death wasn't no more to it than TOC latrine." Which was when Inna Lee slugged Eddie Ivory, her fist catching him on the eye socket, releasing blood enough for the two of them to wipe up.

"Eddie Ivory," she said, "I don't want to hear no more about it."

Thereafter, she had a hard time imagining her husband Coy—which was, she assumed, how true heartache worked in those the victim of it. Once she pulled her wedding album out and flipped through its snapshots like a detective wondering where a clue would appear. This album, she thought, was like her high-school yearbook, Coy no more to her than that pimply know-it-all in geometry class who used to warn of war with Fidel Castro. She read some names: J. D. Summers, Missy Hess, R. W. and Cecil Blackwood, Billie Jean LaTook—wedding guests who seemed as unfamiliar now as those places on the moon which have names. She looked at the presents she'd received way back then as an eighteen-year-old: J. C. Penney gift certificate, three-speed blender, steak knives with real wood handles, seventy-five dollars from Ellen Tharpe. "Well," she said many times, "well, how about this." The only clear memory she had of Coy was the night they had sex, after Homecoming, at Dick and Joe Anderson's house, Coy in the shirt he believed made him look like Johnny Carson. He was already talking about joining Uncle Sam and tried to take it to her as he believed a Marine ought—with much growling and a flurry of handwork. "Hold on," she said, "here, help me out of this." There were a hundred things to take off, it seemed, girdle and beaver-cheaters and real silk hose and those lilac panties she felt so special in. "I couldn't ask for no more than this," Coy said. "That sure is true," she said. Then, seeing her spread out on Mr. and Mrs. Anderson's bed, his face a mostly animal display of thankfulness, he said, "Oh, Jesus. Oh, God."

"When he got on," she told Eddie Ivory, "I was thinking of other things." This was the night Eddie said he wouldn't be coming around any more, there being an attraction on the West Coast he would see about. "I was thinking how much my dress cost and what time it was, and Coy was just sweating and making faces at me below him." She said she stopped thinking entirely when Coy went inside her and there was nothing to do but push back and make the same noises he did. Which were all about love and this tempest they were and being unable to hold back. "I think he went 'oh-oh-oh-oh' and I did the same." Eddie Ivory already had his underpants on and was hunting for his shoes. "He said touch him here and here and kiss him, which I did. I could hear Dick and Joe Anderson in the living room with their dates. They were dancing, Dick singing along with the Rolling Stones." Inna Lee hummed a little for Eddie, that section which talked about having to have it and what the effect is. "Then I had an orgasm, too," she said. She didn't care where Eddie was now, for she was pretty much speaking for herself, saying that in the liquid rush of lights and tingles, because of the fear it wrought, she knew this boy atop her was already dead; it would just take another year or so and maybe fifteen thousand miles between them for Coy to flop down and realize it.

Which is how—at the same instant Burl Perteet was addressing a Dolphin tight end on which point of the spectrum to dream on—love and death became linked in her mind, not to mention fixed to that spot she'd imagined so often: that spot presided over by the friendly shining moon and now soaked with body liquors most of us only read about.

When I woke up, she was studying the picture on my nightstand.

"That's Eva," I said. "She gets 26 percent of everything. Alimony."

Whereupon I heard the foregoing tale of boys named Coy and Eddie, and, surviving it, that female who was here with me. It was a story, I did believe, such as told by drunks about their first pet or lost riches.

"After Coy got off me," she was saying, "I was as wet as you have made me now."

She had eyes which seemed composed of oil and coal.

"Say, why don't I call you sometime?" I said I was going fishing up in Canada with the defensive backfield but would call when I got back. To be true, and I am now ashamed to say so, it was a lie to ease her out of here and my life forever. I should've known.

"Here," I said, "write down your number."

Time moved on as it will in my world, and in August I went into another Baldwin-Wallace training camp, that beef of me much older, my knee-pans held fast by gizmos of stainless steel and miracle fabric; and I thought little about Ms. DuFoys until that afternoon, during two-a-days, when three from the Blue squad, including a lunatic rookie who desired to be the new edition of yours truly, sought to batter old Burl's kidneys and shiver his thinking parts so that number 56 would go down in a pile the size of an economy sedan.

They—Knots Weaver, Mossy Cade, Moe Bias—lined up across from me, each grimy with professional NFL sweats. You could tell they had hearts of fire, plus smug daytime visions of fame.

"Old man," they said, "your time has arrived." They spoke as one, their minds evidently from the same gutter.

Your hero was idle upstairs. He was pooped, what he was, with no hope save that which would later come with rest and one million calories of food.

"Here we come," they snarled.

You're right in thinking they were as savage as Burl Perteet himself had been in the faraway world of his youth.

There was a whistle and in an instant of tremor, crunch and riot, they were atop that man who was me—one muttering "Whoop, whoop, whoop!" in the ear, another chewing the hand, the third babbling of the mists and dim lights of the Great Elsewhere. I had the feeling there were one thousand folks on the sidelines—and in homes across ruined America—going, "Hoot, hoot, hoot!"

"I can't breathe," I gasped. "Honest, it's growing dark down here."

Someone was spitting. There was heard consternation and discouraging language, and your hero felt himself being squashed, sod squeezing into his earhole. I was on the brink, I know now, of a vision of Old Testament proportions—swift, unbidden and full of awe.

"I can't feel my arm," I hollered.

Somebody was pummeling my tender parts.

"I can't feel my leg either!"

And here it was, while flopped down and spread out, that I thought of that woman, Inna Lee DuFoys, and the story she told—a story about a heedless man such as Burl Perteet who might have stood over a naked woman, saying *Oh, God* and *Jesus,* never guessing what awaited in the darksome world of the future.

"Wait," I yelled from the bottom of the mound I was. "Don't be bending my nose, I've got something to say."

One of them, Mossy Cade, was eyeballing me, his face suspicious like what happens at a Mexican rodeo: "What you want to say?"

There were nerve noises in my head: I could imagine Inna Lee as she had been her Homecoming night, that now dead boy of hers flinging himself at her like she was a wall he had to get over. I saw her naked and smiling and pointing to herself, saying, "You don't want to do nothing else, boy. You just want to come on over here and have this and these and all they do stand for."

I was stunned as no Bear or Colt or Ram had ever whacked me.

"Hey," Mossy Cade was saying, "what's wrong with your face, it's crawling!"

I imagined her the night Eddie Ivory visited and her shirt fell open and her eyes said something like "Look what I have to give, give, give." I imagined her skin, which was fine as new money, and her eyes, which were bright and proper places to hide in. And then, an instant before those boys stomped my wits into a blackout, I saw myself just as Inna Lee had seen Coy: bedraggled and flung into a vaster world of woe, flesh forever exiled from a love so fierce it could survive distance, time, even mortal misfortune.

That night the Turk knocked at my door. (The Turk's the beast who bears the bad news—which is usually that you ain't wanted no more or have gone in trade for that which is younger, faster, stronger and cheaper.)

"How you feel about playing in Dallas?" Coach Sam said.

"I could use my option," I said.

"Yes, you could, Burl."

My contract said I could choose: did I want to stay here, a brooding presence pacing the sidelines, or did I want to play sports with blonds from *People* magazine named Lance and Dougie, or did I want to quit?

Which was when I conceived of this woman who is now my wife and what we are here for in this world.

"Coach, I retire."

It took forty minutes for me to pack and be out of there toward her doorstep. I felt as remarkable as I had that afternoon the GM for the Lions phoned and said how'd I like being a number one draft pick, of which there were only eighteen on this planet. This was my thought, exactly: Burl, that thing you see is the future with its arms open and waiting to smother you in luxury. I felt as Coy must've when he shed his Johnny Carson outfit: chosen, powerful and clean as an angel.

I banged on her apartment door at 1:30 P.M. A minute later I'd pitched the other fellow out.

"Miss DuFoys," I said. Yes, I was on bended knee. "Would you marry me?"

She eyed me like I was something dark which she recognized from her past.

I would be generous, I said, would never go off, would carry her around on my shoulders day and night if such pleased.

"Where would we live?"

I was right: she did have a practical mind.

"We can go anywhere," I said.

"I'd like to go home, to Georgia."

That was fine, I said. Budweiser had promised me a beer distributorship, and didn't they drink that stuff down there?

"Please, say yes."

She held her arms apart, and I stumbled into them like one of those halfbacks I'd dispatched in my other life.

"Now, why would I want to do that?" she said. "You tell me."

As I say, this was ages gone. We were married four years ago in the Presbyterian manner, dozens of my erstwhile coworkers in attendance with their tarts, and then we came down here where I stand around in a drafty warehouse ten hours a day, six days a week, and holler at whiskered delinquents named Poot and Joe Bob, or sometimes eat roast chicken and cold peas at a high-school honors athletic dinner. At these events, I get to talk about that which I have little affection for: prowess and how it feels to imperil the other fellow.

We have a toddling girl, Marvine, and one on the way which, if male, will be the Junior of me. We have a swimming pool Esther Williams might like and a rec room such as is favored by Italian movie gangsters. I drive a Ford pickup and can be often seen lost in its wrap-around stereo music; and nothing lifts my heart to a higher point than pulling into my driveway and seeing this woman I love waving to me from the kitchen like I'd been gone years and had to live through wild happenstance to get here.

But you want to know, don't you, what I said to her that night my life took a turn for the splendid item it is now.

What I said was this—the gist of it, at least: I wasn't nothing but overlarge and rewarded for it, a modern monster which lumbered left and right mostly, and did no good except for others' pocketbooks.

I said, "I want to be with you, Inna Lee DuFoys."

I said, "I need that thing you gave your boy Coy."

Yes, I was holding her just as you would hold your own hope if it had heart and leg and tongue.

At last, I said I intended to expire in that spot she imagined so completely—that spot, as I comprehend it now, where I am young and beautiful and eternally loved even though I am dead.

WE GET SMASHED AND OUR ENDINGS ARE SWIFT

Oh, I did love the murder: the life-affirming "Aaaarrrggghhh!" the dying made when they spied the vast What-Not opening to greet them.

First was a cocaine gangster named Wo Tin (Col.), a II Corps Friendly and part-time VC. This was '67—a time you know as distant but dreadful—and I crept upon him like night itself, slipped over the wall of his Frenchy villa, plugged the barrel of That Which Is, my 16, in his nosehole. He smelled like a new car.

"Awake, sleaze," I whispered. "I am here to ease you through the light and into hell." It was a handsome speech. "Think of me as that which hastens and regrets not."

Beside him slept beauty improved upon only by memory: woman. Later, I discovered she was Mai Ming, herself incorrigible for MACV purposes.

"What were you dreaming about, Tin?" I wondered. "I bet it was increase, weal enough to smite with. You were not, for example, picturing woe and wist, right?"

He burst from dreamland, blubbering. "Who you?" he gasped. "You no dipstick!" He was outraged, insulted. "Who you?"

"Herkie Walls," I told him. TCU graduate, interested in Divinity and its Failure. Now in the employ of Uncle Sugar's forces of good. Eyeballs flashing with horror, he was confused. He knew me as an Air America fuck-up, seen hither and yon, harmless. In the moonlight, you could see his shoulders sprinkled with sweat. I was military, I told him, ill-favored and stealthful, my duties the simple business of righting wrongs. I was Superman. "Rise," I said, whereupon we tippy-toed into the adjoining room, him in his gook undies, me in an Abercrombie jungle suit, my gringo face a Halloween mask of night-fighter cosmetic: Avon for the specter in us.

"You wrong," he was yammering. "Wo Tin plenty good guy. VC much death. I spit on NVA. Poot! Poot!"

In the other, finer world, he would have been a plowhorse.

"You want names, I give." He rattled off several, among them many who had been good and were now evil, plus those without courage or keenness. The Colonel's hair looked distressed, itself squalid.

I told him, quietly, "Were my Daddy Ben or brother Buck here, they'd be for abusing you first—having you kneel, snap your arms off at the shoulder. They're indelicate. Me, I think in lofty terms, not laggard."

You could hear that gruesomely attractive Ming stirring, calling out, "Bo Chai, cheri." Wo Tin trembled before me.

In his mind, I was as unwelcome a creature as Godzilla. I pressed That Which Is into his belly. I was cool, as removed from this enterprise as you are from your grunting forefather, Australopithecus.

"I no scare," he was saying. "I top-notch motherfuck." He dropped his pants, showed me his dong. "Big testes, no scare!"

I was amused.

"You scum bag," he said. "Wo Tin is King of valley." He tried to piss on my boots. "Wo Tin is son of God, bring heavy shit down on white man."

"Say bye-bye to me, Colonel," I hissed. "Say bye-bye to toot and appetite and such. Say hello, instead, to leaving this vale of etceteras."

"How long you been fool?" he said, aghast. "King not impressed."

It was then, while he sputtered and flapped his arms, that I divided him from the sum of his parts, vaporized his angers and loves and spites, and splattered a thousand ounces of his flesh and vitals against a wall. Ah, rapture. Ah, folly.

My mentor was Major Veloy T. Vigil, to murder what wingedness was to Victory, or E. Pound to verse. He picked me at Benning, in Georgia, where I walked around with a beret and believed I knew what I was doing. He saw in me, he said, vitality, a quality identified as Supreme and Refined. I was material, he said. He could give shape to my pain. He could make me a bona fide Furtivo living on the loose and exciting ends of things.

"You in love?" he said.

I was. Wasn't all youth?

"Margo is a Tri-Delt," he said. "Her legs are—here the report is quite specific—*golden* and *slim.*"

We were standing in a grenade pit, the occasion an exercise in concussion. "I know everything about you, Walls." He had the look of an animal that had been through a dozen mates. "Your favorite color, the way you prefer potatoes, how you sleep with women—I know and approve."

"So what?" I said. "I'm a primate that can think a little. Impress me."

"You've read Bethe and Hubble, cared for neither." He stared downrange, to where the howling came from. This was an operation the brass called Mind and Matter. "You like having and keeping it, plus making it last. You desire—"

"—I like finding it for myself," I declared. "Daddy Ben taught me how—by being diligent and witty."

"Your daddy is a caveman," he said. "I'll be your daddy now. Here."

He thrust on me a sheet of camp stationery. *Dear Margo,* it read, *Marry somebody else, perhaps that Jeeter. He's fine, I suppose, and what this world deserves in the way of citizens. Also, burn my letter sweater; football fails to interest any longer. What excites now is sentiment and action. Sell my guitar; I've no need for the uplift of staff and clefnote. If you choose to wait, look for me in a few years; I'll be the one smiling and full of glory. You were wonderful to me, bye.*

"What's in this for me?" I said.

"Knowledge, boy, and a way in the world. Let's go, Herkie Walls, let's go see us the light."

I went, I told him later, 'cause of loneliness, plus an orphan's desire to please.

At many places, he trained us—DeFuniak Springs (Florida), Camp Vicars (Philippines), Langley. We were two: your sympathetic hero and Zion T. McKinney, a Buffalo spade. Zion had virtually homosexual hair, complex and meaningful, public enough to be a monument to usury and pride.

"There's awe in my background," he told me when we met. "I'm collegiate, too. Ask me about thought and how it works in those that suffer."

The Major said we were Batman and Robin; or, if we preferred, Alpha and Omega. Zion said we were neighboring links on the Great Chain of Being, abstract enough to be angels but still imperfect enough to be in the rueful business of living and dying.

"I want you boys to dwell in the cheery half of the spectrum," the Major said. "Think not of fruity coughs and body liquors; think of serving Uncle Sugar and Mr. Johnson." He gave us many friendly whacks on the hind parts. "Lord, this is a fine moment."

In the following months, the Major took us the length and breadth of stalking, pouncing, doing America's duty and living to tell about it. We learned to tippy-toe, to creep, to shimmy through tiny holes, to dash like a thug, and to ape affection for the common joys. Using charts and color graphs and texts like *Building the Perfect Beast,* a War College anthropologist taught us native squats, habits of mind to use in the badlands, the difference among drools, and where the self comes from. We learned ordnance, code and the shortest path to reward. For a time, life was knowledge and the palaver to express it. We could do call of bird, bark of dog, and lovers' method of moil.

"Shit fire!" Zion said once, "compared to this, Tuskegee was a nursery. Man, we are in the realm of allegory and hard science."

We learned to kill, of course. I could usher a being out with matchbook, school tie or NuTonic golf spikes. One time, in the wrestling room at Wright Pat AFB, I dropped the Major and threatened him with his own lips. "Major," I said, "consider yourself eviscerated."

"Aaaarrrggghhh," he said. smiling.

In another exercise, Zion and I went round and round, he the hero, I the hood. I had, at my disposal, a bio of cunning and double-dealing, plus a pair of sassy underlings to make life easy. Zion had craft and a 1300 on his SATs.

"I could have gotten you with bomb, ring full of poison, or wily female," he said. We were standing at a make-believe street corner, a hundred phony civilians ambling nearby. "Instead, I will take you with this."

He showed me a toenail, sharp as a barong, then incapacitated me with a deadly move involving ears, thighs, and my own optimism.

"I'm disappointed," the Major said. "He could have done the deed with a Greek toga."

In the last stages of our training, we made a weapon of the metaphysical. Stoicism, foresight, the cynical—Zion and I handled them as expertly as we flung blunts from our Jetfire .25s. In our capable hands, human dirts, melts and sighs became as murderous as commando dagger or piano wire. "Watch this," Zion said once. His face lit by joy, he slew a make-believe villain with two Sugar Bowl tickets and pressure applied to the site of the soul. "Not bad," I said, "take notes." I delivered my opponent into Never-Never land, using only the Knights of Columbus motto and a Sitting Bull metaphor addressing the masses and the poets who lead them. Zion and I felt select and Spartan—already part of the next epoch of humans. "Man, I feel splendid," Zion said. "Ain't we moving between the jaunty and superb!"

"I can do no more," the Major said later. "If there's a heap, you're atop it. Below you is rubble."

We were meeting in a spy-mobile, a 1965 Fairlane, yellow over black. It was night, of course, and we sat in the parking lot of a grit bar called the Sulphur Inn. This was the Florida panhandle, summer and the sweats upon us.

"I am proud," Vigil was saying. Rangy, with skin like saddlecloth, he looked like a redneck named Joe Ben or Mookie; you couldn't tell he was a Baylor Ph.D., single-handedly responsible for Korea. "From now on, everything's real. You've the ability and the frame of mind. You've the words: spathaceous, puissant, griseous. Go and succeed."

Then he gave us our assignments, each in an EYES ONLY security pouch. Mine was Wo Tin; Zion's a Syrian specimen named Ahmed "Bronco" Majd, specialist in humbug and illicit doody.

In time, Zion and I began working together. In '68 we sneaked up-country in Cambodia, found an ingrate coconut monk named Su Lin "Teddy" Ky. We passed ourselves off as illiterate GIs, AWOL grunts seeking asylum in any of the available promised lands. "Big damn dollar," Su Lin said, "You got damn dollar, huge size, you go Danish place. Teddy do miracle with moola." We slew him with mysticism and angina-producing root juice. His face turned purple and his tongue looked like a cauliflower. "Buddha snatched that sucker up," Zion told Ky's minions. "Let us pray for your round and mortal dude."

We zapped a Thai gun merchant with arguments swiped from Luther and Erasmus. We told him we were Treasury dicks, in Bangkok on the trail of sin.

"No dig," he said. He wore clothes like an hour-old sunburn. "I got girls. You come back later. Say hi Wanda. Say hi Mickey Monkey. Everybody lay flat and be nasty."

Zion, face blue as a prizewinner's ribbon, stuck a work of Reformation doctrine against the man's throat. We watched the man's Adam's apple bob like a fishing float.

"You want hop?" The Thai held a stick of dried vegetable matter. "Plenty good stuff. Take you new world. You see Chubby Checker. You see sun, moon, all stars in space. Old world no good for you."

Soon after this Zion's dreams began. "Lord to God!" he said after the first. We were in a two-star safe house near Do Long, Zion upright in bed, his face as empty as a two-quart soup bowl. His nightmare had been classic—full of soils, movie-house snakes and long tumbles into darkness. "Shit, I don't want to go in there again," he said. "It was fear, Herkie. Let's stay awake forever." The next dream featured us in an era of unbecoming flail and thrash. "Maybe I'm being told something," Zion said. "It's my racial memory, that's what." In another, he met himself coming out a door, his face as eerie as the bottom of the sea. "Herkie," he said, "you know those ugly fish with the eyes?" I did. "I'm them," he said. "Let's drink, okay?"

In the fall, before we were to return to the States, the Major ordered us to hit a proto-datu Filipino mucky-muck named Lazar. He was inept, we were told, in the way of the tidy and swift result. Lazar stood between America and rapture.

"Count me out," Zion said. "I'm weary. Let's stop in Hawaii, do a thing with females."

We were in Subic Bay, a secure BOQ, our wish a command to those from the homely class.

"One more time," I said. "Then we go in the sunshine, rest and recreate."

"I wasn't raised to be this." He lay in his skivvies, reading a volume on *modernismo,* the drift toward undoing. Mine was *The Kingdom of Leather,* an LA mystery with a tasteful ending. "You should've seen me as a youngster," he was saying. "I got pictures. I was a wonderful infant. Look at this face. Ain't it a work?"

"Me, too," I said. "I was always an attraction."

"My momma had expectations for me." He was shaking his head, that recondite hair of his sloshing back and forth like liquid in a box. "Heartbreak wasn't one of them."

"Think vacation," I suggested. "Lapping waters, strong drink, wahinis."

"I'm thinking on Velva. She's my hometown girl. She's— what?—hank and bone. Damn, her kisses'll take the parch out of you."

"Fret not," I said. "The Major owes us a break. We've been stellar."

Zion's face said, *Man, I just want to lay on the shores of Erie and live me the life.* You could tell he was thinking of leisure and aging in the proper manner.

"Listen," I said, putting my book down. I'd gotten to the part about the gaudy tree spirits and six hours of whiskey. I touched Zion on the arm. Despair brought out the tactile in me. "We'll get us some hooch." I said. "Golden Wedding Bourbon. Run amuck in it, what say?"

"Okay," he shrugged. "My head's in this, my heart's not. It's in another place, dig?"

Lazar's three-storey abode was on Moro Street on the western edge of Manilla, and we approached it like citizens named Ike and Floyd. Our driver, a DAO technician, had a face that resembled an odious state of mind. Juvenescence maybe. You could smell him, too, metallic and stale like well-water. His specialty was finding and fleeing.

"Here it be," he said. "It was nice meeting you, but I'm gone now."

He pitched himself from the Fiat and hurried up the street like a man hunting his only child. Lazar's place, shaded by leafy banyan trees, sat back from the street, protected by a shoulder-high brick fence pink enough to be a granny's powdered cheek.

"Cake," I said. "Candy from you-know-who."

"We go in, blast the fool and are gone, right?" Zion was sweating like a wheel of cheese. "I mean, no lingering this time. We lingered in Qui Nhon. Lingering's not healthful."

"The way I see it, " I began, "we're in and out. Like a cat."

"What kind?"

I regarded heaven. "A big one. A panther."

"A nasty one," he said.

"An English-speaking panther that drives a tank."

Quickly, we ran down our checklist: stealth, ability to hold breath, righteous point of view, months of practice and self-denial. You could hear bug sounds and random residential noise. It was an hour after dusk, the twilight humid and heavy.

"What's that smell?" Zion said. "That's an omen, ain't it? Smells like old poon."

I checked the walkie-talkie. *"Almighty, Almighty, this is Street Gang, do you copy?"*

"Remember," Zion was saying, "it's gone." He had his sweater up, pointing to his breast. "Here, feel."

He snatched my hand to his chest. Ker-thump. Ker-thump.

"Street Gang, this is Almighty. Life is easy. Do it."

Fifteen minutes passed before we left the vehicle, scurrying forth in the commando crouch, eyeballing the yonder and nearabout for that unexpected visitor or untoward noise. Strangely, I felt clumsy and uncertain, as if, in leaving the security of our automobile, I had left behind the meat and sense of me, and what was now creeping onward was only a column of bones and profound silliness.

"Zion," I said, "touch my head. Am I hot or what?"

I was nothing, he said, just anxious and overworked, like himself. "In the next life," he said, "I'm coming back as a boss. You can have the fucking proletariat."

I agreed. We weren't but advanced teenagers, still gangly underneath our adult outerwear.

"Why'd you join the Army?" I wondered.

The usual reasons, he said: higher calling and too much time on the hands.

"I went for direction," I whispered. "Before this, I was that slack sort. I lacked spirit. I liked to lay around in my room and brood. One day I looked up and a year had gone by."

Silhouetted in a corner window on the second floor was Lazar, evidently gazing into the gloom and thick night air.

"Man, is he beef or what?"

"The file says he's three hundred pounds of so-and-so. Inspired. You can tell he's mean."

"I'm mean, too," Zion said. He was fingering his Georg Luger. It had a custom barrel which took the .45 ACP cartridge. "On the scale, I'm a ten. Nine's God."

Like fairy-tale beasts, we crept through the gate, scampered through the garden, leaf growth barely crackling under our feet. I had a Randall-22, thirty shells in a clip, fast as a cobra. "I'm an eleven," I said. "I got flair." I could imagine the shredding Senor Lazar would make.

"In here," Zion said.

A window was open and we slipped inside, each in lampblack and late-movie turtlenecks. I could have been a sleek Charles Boyer, Zion equally famous and svelte but Negro.

"Is your God helpful or tricky?" I said.

"Both," Zion whispered. "I fear and love him, honest."

That room was a warehouse of wicker and brass doodads. I was touched: clearly, Lazar was a gent with an eye for the smart and everlasting. There were towels from the Sheraton, crates of Adidas gym shoes, boxes of Planter's Peanuts, electronics from Texas Instruments. He had books, too: *The Rules of the Secular Franciscan Order, Pudd'nhead Wilson*, an issue of *Food Monitor*. I had him figured for an eight. I was wrong.

"Make a noise," I said. "We're punks, remember. In the morning, we should be described as intruders."

"It's not too late," he said. "We could duck out, say we were feebs."

He had a quarterback's smile, loose and expensive.

"The file says he responds to the name King Daddy."

I could hear a chair scrape overhead, then heavy foot-steps. "Go," I hissed. Zion took his position at the doorway which gave onto the entry leading to the stairs. I crawled past him, put myself at the end of the hall. The ambush would be enfilade, a deadly crossfire of wit and true misery.

"I don't hear him," Zion said. "Let's split."

I lay in the shadows, the wood floor cold and glossy with wax. The house was quiet, a silence so impacted it had weight and shape and spook-house mystery. I could already imagine Major Vigil congratulating us. I felt lifted, I did, as tenuous and fine as victory itself.

"I'm weak," Zion was saying. "You didn't see my charts. I'm in the dip places, Herkie. Imagine the writing Hebrews have. That's my philosophy, Herkie: I go backwards and am also black inside."

The files said Lazar was ponderous, slow-witted as an ape, ruthless. Said he dealt in disregard. Said he couldn't be taken with pith nor wish nor esoterica.

"What's called for," I told Zion, "is bullet power and true aim."

"Did you hear me dreaming last night?" Zion said. "I was appalled. You were in it, too. We were dancing. I had an evening gown, a hibiscus in my hair. You were the Abominable Snowman. What a disappointment."

You could hear nothing from above—not squeak, not creak, not thump of heart.

"You know what my middle name is?" Zion whispered. "It's Spot. Dig it, I was named after my momma's dog. It was a rude animal. Mangy. Not the least bit delightful."

"Mine's LaVerne," I said. "After an auntie."

From the top of the stairs, I heard a noise, as if a fat enemy

of truth were there trying to make up his mind. My heart gave an ugly lurch sideways, and I felt my ribs close around it like a claw. Calm, I told myself, you are well trained. I went down my list of resources: strong legs for running, clear lungs, a young fool's belief in right and wrong.

"Spot bit my nose once," Zion was saying. "He was a mongrel. Part poodle."

It was then I heard a pssst-pssst-pssst and saw the shiny teak floor explode in front of me. I learned later that Lazar was using a special Wop machine pistol fitted with a silencer. Holes burst into the wall above and to the right. I felt my glands kick in, the effect swift and consummate. It was a preconscious horror: there'd be this effete, pussy piss noise, then a flurry of wallboard debris.

"Scum, Filth, Jerk," Zion was hollering. It was Army textbook, lingo designed to befuddle and delay. The light was catching his face in an odd, obscene way. "Up yours, King Daddy! You're dealing with an honor student!"

More bullets chewed the floor in front of me—fsssst, fssst, fssst—then I heard Zion say "I'm hit" the way you and I say "Howdy." I was scrunched against the door, a turtle looking for a shell.

"Where?" I said.

"Arm, I think. Shoulder, maybe."

Several shots raked the wall to my left, splinters falling in a shower.

"What?" I said.

"I said it doesn't hurt much. Vigil was right; it's annoying but not a true bother."

Warm nerve sparklers sputtered in my brain. Somewhere above us, Lazar was yelling in Arabic. I recognized a couple of words, both having to do with urp and rot. Once, in English, he appealed to his internalisms, froths and meats, for strength. You could hear him puffing, changing clips, shell casings rattling on the floorboards like marbles. Lights were going on everywhere. On and off. I heard a radio—a slope combo doing a brassy tune about doom and loving you.

"I'm pinned," I said. "The Major didn't say nothing about this."

Zion was chuckling. "Know what I'm thinking about?"

"Fug," I said. "That's all I can say. It's the only word in my mind. Fug, fug, fug."

Zion squeezed off a burst. "I was thinking about this track coach I once had. Mirmainian. What a jerk. I was fleet, Herkie, a great finisher. One time he coldcocked me, took me out with some Golden Gloves sucker punch. When I came to, he told he'd been wanting to do that from the first day. Said I was a snide bastard. Said I wasn't mink-shit to him."

"Piss," I said. "I'm thinking of that. Piss and fug."

The smell in that hall was outrageous, wax and wood and cordite.

"We got to get out of here, Herkie. I wasn't raised to be a dead thing."

Sweat-drenched, I was cold, my jaw sore from teeth-gnashing. Lazar sprayed us again, slugs slamming into the plaster: whump-whump, whump-whump. I noticed a wood splinter the size of a tongue depressor sticking out of my sneaker. "Jesus," I said. I yanked it out, bringing with it urp and pulp that looked like part of my toe. Vigil was right: pain was just a thing pantywaists fussed about.

"Give me cover, Zion. I'll go out the door, come up from behind."

Another tune was playing, this one about bad sex. It used the Spanish phrase *noche obscura.*

"Negative," my pal said. "Bring the car around back. Look for me in five. I'll be the one running."

Above, Lazar huffed like the Big Bad Wolf. I heard him mention angry mountain gods and pigs, then Zion's piece went off, and I felt at one with thought and being.

"Go, Herkie, goddammit!"

Quick-time, I rolled hard, grabbed the door handle, and dived out. "Whip up! Get some!" Zion was yelling. I was charging through the tangled garden in a fury. I was at the stage before thought, the one of bone and thirst, hormone and electricity. Once a low-hanging branch whacked me in the chin. It was another second before I realized it was raining, fiercely and in thick, air-sucking sheets. I could hear nothing behind—neither gunfire nor cries of agony. Whoa, I said to myself when I hit the street. To anybody looking out, Harold, you should be only another idiot without an umbrella. Once in the car, I lay on the front seat, pulling myself together, gathering my parts from the various horrors they'd been in. Lazar's house was dark now.

"Almighty, Almighty," I said into the walkie-talkie. "Almighty, this is Street Gang. Come in." There was only static and the rustle of deepest space. "Almighty, come the fuck in!" It was code for that celebrated fan with the stuff on it.

Around back, I counted the minutes in the old-timey way: one–Mississippi, two–Mississippi. I was crying, too, my face a smear of tears and snot. I couldn't breathe, and my heart was all over the world—throat, small of back, dribbling down my leg. Shit, I kept saying. Shit. I could hear the Major talking to me. "Guts, boy," he was saying, "skill, foresight, ability to organize—you got 'em, now use 'em. Convert this present heartache to lasting advantage."

Then I saw Zion. He was running—not toward me, but away, his wounded arm limp like an orangutan's.

"Ain't I natty?" he said when I pulled the Fiat abreast. His face had madness all through it. "Herkie, this is one speedy spade!"

Rain poured off him. Talking looked like spitting.

"Get in." The floorboard on my side was a pool of water and blood. Toe, I thought, you will be missed. "Let's go, Zion. C'mon, we're out of this thing in grand style."

"Wrong." A fierce light was in his eyes. You could see in him aggravation and panic and pride. "You go," he said. "I'm finished."

Ahead was a Shell station and storefronts, an extraordinary display of ricketyness. Our whole world was constructed from corrugated tin and chicken wire and the heavy cardboard fatty foods are shipped in; our whole world was the simple elements: water, light, fear.

"Quit later," I said. "We're expected. Let's drink and forget."

He stopped. Wheezing, a sucking sound coming from somewhere as the rain washed over his mouth, he leaned against the Fiat. I felt antsy, on the edge of this or that. Don't snivel, I thought.

"Herkie Walls," he said, touching my face, "forget me. Say I died. Tell the Major I vanished."

A chill shot through me. There was nothing humanoid in his face. I could have been talking to a chair.

"What about—?"

"Herkie Walls, you were fine," he said. "And I liked you very much."

Then he was gone, darting from the car, disappearing into the streaks and swirls of night-rain as if he'd slipped through the seam between one shadow and the next.

The Major was aggrieved, his voice in that hard place between whine and howl. In his civvies—Gucci loafers, Lacoste golf shirt, Foster Grants—he resembled a man with a dozen foul ideas. He might have been cholera with legs.

"I felt it," he was saying, "in here." He thumped his gut. "I told the old lady, Millie, that something was going wrong. That my boys were holding the soiled end of the you-know-what."

We were in the isolation ward at Beaumont in Ft. Bliss, Texas, my injured foot bandaged to the calf. I was getting strong home-vibes from the sharp sunlight and the knowledge that outside my window lay a baked, extreme landscape, a desert of hot soils, prickly pear and cruel, shiny bird. It was such an endless stretch of zeroness that in it, humping through on foot or Jeep, you felt clean and eternal. Thought dropped away like old skin and you became slime or angel. You had wings or scales and, thankfully, you knew nothing about that which interrupted the necessary march from urge to action.

"What'd we lack?" The Major was shaking his head. "Nerve, guile, what? We had the intentions, which were choice. We have everything—penicillin, cable TV, Cutty Sark. You tell me."

"What happened to King Daddy?"

The Major stopped pacing at the end of the bed, looked mournfully at my upraised and still tender foot.

"He went down the next day," he said. "Locals did the cleanup. Went in as janitors or some such. Separated him from the earthly coil, so to speak. It was very wet."

He showed me several photos, glossy 8-x-10s of defeat and carnage.

"And Zion?"

I could feel the heat outside, close and still and permanent, the heat of heat itself—the white, wool-thick heat from one hell I've heard described.

"Skedaddled," the Major was saying. "You know, I hated that son of a bitch. Honest. You should have seen his P-Profile. Truly, it was a map of the unlovely. I thought I could turn him around, put him on the high road. He had it all—the suppressions, the depressions, the tendencies. His blot test was an education." Where others had seen elephants, the Major said, Zion has seen the boogeyman or a notion like love given the shape of a pterodactyl.

"When do I leave here?" I asked. "I've the need to go home for a time."

Vigil was fingering the PX goodies he'd brought, a Sony tape deck and a handful of Otis Redding cassettes. I felt for him the emotion that in the ordinary mind often stands next to sorrow: pity.

"I had that so-and-so to the quarters once," he said. "Millie did her usual fine work on the kitchen front. Zion was appreciative, I thought, deeply so. Apparently, I was wrong. It was just an early stage of malingering. Henceforth, I am prepared for the worst."

"Send that nurse in, will you? I desire a drug."

After he left, I took a substance and abandoned the present agitation for an ocean of listlessness.

For six months, I lay in my Daddy Ben's house in Goree, Texas, letting the training and promise drain out of me. Vigil was right: Daddy Ben was a caveman. He was uglier than I remembered, his brow a shelf of wrinkled, gray flesh. His eyes held nothing but the need to make it, spend it, eat it, or play with it till it died. My brother Buck was no comfort either. Once we went out, to the Mile 49 Bar. It was pure shitkicker, the band an over-brained bunch called The Aggie Ramblers. Everything they did—tunes and what tunes stand for—had a whang and tug to it, including a special version of "All Hail the Power." The Ramblers paid lavish attention to the part that addressed avarice and temporary pleasures. We watched an hour, then I told Buck to take me home. I could smell myself, ripe and musty both. Also, I had the markings of an AAA criminal's beard, hairs in curious pattern on my neck.

"It's nothing personal," I told Buck. "It's funk. I'll emerge wiser, stronger."

"What happened to you?" he said. "You used to be a fun guy."

"I used to be a dipstick," I told him. "I used to be a dorkface."

Beginning the first week, the Major called me every day. His code was Pericles; mine, the Wanderer. He sent me the dossiers of miscreants and villains, often three and four in a bundle marked GLASS—HANDLE WITH CARE. They were an amazing lot, these bad guys, their specialties jeopardy and common subversion: Cong, Pathet Lao, PLO grits, a Brussels fag named Rene.

"I got one here you'll love," the Major announced once. "He's vain, you could do him with bombast. You ought to see the way he puts it away then takes it out again. What say, Harold? Let's drop you in his life."

That week I looked at a Lagos mercenary who had the worldview of a raccoon that could rhyme a little Latin. It was a photo of him and several beauties, each of whom appeared to be having political thoughts.

"You got to work," the Major said. "Get back in the flow. You've a high brain getting slack."

Another time, Pericles wanted to chopper me into Venezuela, deliver a nasty birthday surprise to a Colonel identified as The Puma of Santa Cruz. I could slip in as the Peace Corps idealist, do the business, then vamoose. The DEA would love me as nuns love God.

"Send another," I said. "This sounds Ivy League. Maybe Big Ten. *Buckeye* is the word on my tongue."

The dossiers kept piling up: turncoat, double-dealer, aggressors of the usual ilk. What makes a man bad, I wondered. Was it genes or being raised wrong? Maybe it was diet or having dreams. What happens to a man who eats lettuce and wants to be happy? We are mud, I thought, or we are not.

I slept in issue-jamies, my dreams flights into the faraway and long-ago. I drank hooch, Buds foremost, and once, in the company of "I've Got a Secret" on TV, brought time itself, like Daddy Ben's pickup, to a dead halt. My thoughts were fragrant, even rewarding. I could see backwards and forwards, with equal clarity, to the flat dry Eden we come from and aim to go to.

"Herkie Walls," I said at last, "you ought to get a job. Roughnecking, maybe. You'd make somebody a dandy employee." And I thought so often of Margo, my old sweetie, that my heart did a tight spin on its own root.

Then the word on Zion started trickling in.

"He's been seen here and there," the Major said. "He's gone over, I believe, become a creature of chaos."

Zion's disguises were masterful: importer, Frog Writer ("with a gift for trope and indirect statement"), person with all the hope out of him. In one report, he was both grizzled and smooth. Another said he trafficked in the semi- and fully precious. The best, filed by a field officer named Krebs, said Zion was moving between thought and realization. There was a note, too: *Vigil,* it read, *I am in a place beyond the petty and day-to-day. Maybe you want to come in here with me. I have left your business for mine, which is living and being free. Come ahead, Vigil, I am jubilant. P.S. Tell Herkie my last dream was about flowers and easeful loves.* His hidey-hole was Saigon, a Tu Do street beauty parlor named the White Lakes.

"What'll it be?" the Major said. "You and me this time. It's our bird, our nest."

"I think not," I said.

"You're making me sad, Herkie."

"Convince me," I said. "I am content here."

"For the beauty of it. Think of tying up a loose string. This is the only smudge on an otherwise immaculate record. Listen, I've got our covers picked out." We were to be layabouts named Punk and Ace. I was to be the former, crafty and street-smart as those in America's ghettos.

Something snapped together for me in that instant: we

cannot round the world from within; we have limits and must know them. Plus: we are dogs with the might of angels.

"Okay," I said. "I lead. You can be the one carrying the bags."

That afternoon I visited Margo.

"What do you want?" she said.

I was shaved and sweetened, a cloud of Jade East like a halo over my ears. She was as I recalled her—my succulent and fully realized female: love that had hair and skin and hot parts to cling to. My heart went to my throat like a plug.

"Where's Jeeter?"

He was a dullard, she said, more interested in the longed-for than the real. He liked to stay up late and talk about college.

"Why are you here? What do you want from me?"

I aimed to lay on top of her. Or her on top of me. The positions didn't matter.

She looked sly. "Why should I want to do that?"

As Zion had done—now years ago, it seemed—I pointed to my chest. There was a heart, I said, which needed a warm item against it. I wanted her next to me, upright or supine. I desired stroking, an activity that would transport the both of us. I wanted many quakes, I told her, shudders that culminated in the fabled rush of insight and knowledge. "Let's whoop together," I said. "I'm in a generous mood."

For an instant, her eyeballs remained dark with suspicion, then she smiled and I lurched toward her, weak-kneed and blind with bliss.

"Does this mean we're engaged again?" she said.

Truly. I had only one duty left; then, for better or worse, she'd be mine, I hers.

"There are a thousand kinds of love," I whispered. "I believe this is one of them."

We, the Major and I, hung outside the alley door to the White Lakes. We were those Grimm Brothers wolves you know and wonder about: sparkly eyeteeth and deformed with belief. Inside we heard a voice, feminine. It was discussing its underclothes.

"You got to be big in there," the Major was saying. His face was a work of hunger and exile. His parents could have been large trees. "Look at me, Herkie. I'm part Mex, part something else, Jew maybe. I'm small also. Compact. Nevertheless, inside I'm gigantic."

"Me, too," I said. "I wish I could show you."

Here, in that alley, the sunlight was biblical—gladsome and renewing, a light to shine on heroes everywhere. I felt a flood of fine feelings, many of them having to do with humans.

"This is not one thing we're doing," the Major said. "It's many things."

I had my weapon out, a SIG 9mm, a tiny instrument capable of serious wrath.

"I'll give you two minutes." Vigil was dressed for business, an ecru velveteen jumpsuit and glamour-girl makeup. I was reminded of something flossy and playful. "You go in, do your duty, exit with a grin. We've others to cover the tracks."

Just then the woman came out. It was, of course, Ming, Colonel Wo Tin's sleep partner. She was svelte and no doubt a toothsome morsel to those of that mind. Neat, I thought. We'd come full circle.

"Don't worry," I told her. She was on the C list, a minor target. We'd get to her had we the necessary hour and a way of hurting her first. "You go on home," I said, "we youth in America are a forgiving kind."

She gave me an unloving look, then disappeared into the vermin and hoo-rah that was Tu Do Street. I felt nothing for her—neither nostalgia nor concern nor a yearning to be intimate.

"I'm Presbyterian," Vigil was saying. "We believe in doing and reflecting afterwards."

"Touch my arm."

He grabbed me above the wrist, his eyes adrenal and mad with homicide.

"That's the cool of a man full of his mission," I said. "You wander in there in a minute. See what awaits."

"Damn, Herkie, I love you." I believed he might weep. "In this life, you had the wrong daddy, truly. I told Millie you were a son and a credit. Sugar is proud, LBJ is proud, Veloy Vigil is proud. Smile, Herkie, you're on the verge."

Inside, I found Zion. His place was an empire of contraband and Free Enterprise booty: doohickey, geegaw, widget. Floor to ceiling, it was warehouse and whoosis inferno: TVs, Raleigh racers, Whirlpool appliances, liquors, rubber clothes, Kung Fu movies. He was meeting every taste and secret need, and I was not surprised. In the middle, like one king Milton wrote about, sat Zion, still teeth and animal eye movement, wearing a Colpro safari jacket and shorts. His throne brought to mind the words *dynasty* and *serf*. I resisted the urge to haul myself into his lap.

"What happened to your hair?" It was no longer epic.

"Modern times," he said. "Ming calls this the style of the future."

He was bald, his skull a diamond of glints.

"I like it," I said.

He told me he'd improved his mind, too, done for his understanding of the workaday what he'd done to his appearance. "My brain's a well-folded mass, Herkie. I've put a fine edge on it. I'm sharp now." He was living on the unvexed, moonlit place of this life, he explained, himself the product of joycraft and unstinting self-examination. "What kind of weapon you carrying?"

I put it on the table. Jesus, it was a shameful machine, pure cop show.

"You got room for another?" I said. "I'm considering retirement."

He looked at me as though I was as useless as a hubcap on a tractor.

"Why you want to do that?" he said. "Out here, with me, there's nothing but sport and the living of it."

"I know something," I said, "Let's you and me be cohorts. We could swipe a boat, float up the Mung River. Let's be on the same side of the fence again, Zion. I'm tired of the indoor life."

He shook his gleaming head a dozen times and the air went right out of me.

"Don't," he said. "Do the deeds you're paid for."

Here it was that Major Vigil dashed in. He was lip-breathing, his eyes yellow and angry lights. "Kiss it off, Zion!" he hollered. Moving monkeylike, he scooted to Zion's side. "You let me down, son. I lost sleep and face and—what else did I lose, Herkie?"

The Major was a presence like no other I'd noticed in this world. He was might and skill, character and fuss. I was impressed.

"You took the low road, Zion," he was saying. "Unhappy things happen on that road. I'm one of them."

"I know that road," I said quietly. Death organs had given way inside of me—lungs and guts and beating thing. "I know its chuckholes and sewers and where the ruts come from."

All the shine left Vigil's cheeks. "Whaaa—?"

I had picked up my piece. It would look fine, I was thinking, against his nose or on that part of the noggin where the self sits. In my brain were millions of half-things, each ranked and watchful. I expected to look around in a minute and see, well, griffins and hobgoblins—winged, dragon-eyed witnesses from the ghoul-world that have brought us disease and low-mindedness and loam that walks upright.

"You shoot him," I said, "I shoot you." A pulse beat feverishly on his neck. "You'd make a dazzling mist, Major."

He looked as dry as a ditch weed. "I'm confused," he said. His face went toward terror, came back. "Help, help."

"Excuse me," Zion was saying, already half out the room. "I'm gone."

He was right: this was between Vigil and me. Always.

"How about a hug, Zion, for the friends we are?"

He came forward with a smile and lit me up with a clasp anyone's daddy would be proud of. I wanted to kiss him on the cheek and say adios the way cowboys do. Then he was drifting away and gone, and the Major had my full attention.

"Are you dissatisfied, Herkie?" he said. "Haven't I been decent to you?"

I heard something pop in his insides. I knew I had a darling speech if I could remember it. A motorcycle roared to life in the alley. That would be Zion, I thought. In minutes, he will be free and in the arms of, yup, zest.

"I am astounded," the Major was saying. He'd back-pedaled three steps, his face crazed and busy. You could see the purple marks expectation had made. "This is a disappointment, Herkie. A half-hour ago, I was a gay man; now, I feel pitiful."

There is no economy in lust, I told him. Particularly that for death.

"Some people aren't going to be happy about this," he said. "What will you tell them?"

I thought of a thousand things, each impossible as history's many gods.

"I am betrayed," he was muttering. "Well, live and learn, yes?"

I felt almost as I had those many, many months ago when I stood over Wo Tin. Then I had been well down Mister Darwin's artfully conceived tree. I was ooze itself, probably—protein and ruminating mud. Now, watching the Major creep out of that room, I was one of the fully evolved creatures, all arm and leg of me, something that fled the large and permanent NO for the itch and wiggle and plentiful struggle of the YES. I was truly big.

To be true, they captured me, scolded me for months and then threw me back to Texas where I write from now and where ugliness is what Mother Nature grows as weeds. Margo brings me news of the big world. And sometimes, yes, the Major visits. He's considering leaving the service, evidently preferring Millie and her garden of jonquils and lilacs in Florida to the "Ugghh!" and fright of his career. Even Mirmainian, Zion's old track coach, has changed.

I found the man in his gym office. Sweat had turned the walls green.

"Geez," he said, "you're ugly. What happened to your face?"

It was a disguise, I told him. Underneath, I was as beautiful as the next person.

"Hey, I like you. Sit down."

He looked Greek—tired and cynical.

I told him I was on my way to prison. Or home.

"Huh?"

Then I went for him, flipped him onto the concrete floor, using a dance of teeth, thigh and belt loop. It was sophisticated.

"Uh-uh-uh-uh," he was saying.

I gripped him by the ears. "From now on," I said, "I want to hear that you're nice, okay?"

So that's how it is. Margo and I plan a nation of babies, all of whom shall be educated as I was—through error and trial. Visit us, if you like. We have nowhere to go and nothing to call us away from our current life of loving and getting old.

STAND IN A ROW AND LEARN

When I knew him, everybody called him Ears (on account of the obvious), but his true name was Doyle Eugene Wingo and he preferred to speak of himself in the third person, his voice a mostly singsong instrument of twang and nosework. "Doyle Wingo," he'd say, "he's a special guy. You shouldn't mess with him. Mister Charles'll learn that." That day we got off the bus from Deming, New Mexico, at Ft. Bliss for Basic, he told the DI that Wingo, Doyle E., ex–Chapter President of the Banditos, had several distinguished talents, among them higher brain power than most, durability to absorb deprivation of any ilk, and skills at shifting in and out of a Given Brouhaha. You just knew he was going to die in the low place they were certain to send us.

To be true, as I've since told my wife Audrey Jean, Ears was a profound screwup. Soon after we got our greens and tidy haircuts, he went AWOL with Gibbs and Rocky

Perteet, laid waste to a Juarez strip joint called the Cavern—the kind of place, Ears said, you can naturally expect at the convergence of foul water, abused privilege and an economy that caters to unhappy appetites. "Doyle Wingo's educated," he said the next day. "Trust him, he's gifted in these things." He was in the middle of what appeared to be nearly twelve thousand punishment push-ups, his fatigues sweat-stained, his face a pulp of bruises and lumps. "You should have seen your hero," he said. "He was offended, leapt into a dozen greasers." His face took on the shine of a man with moola and new transportation. "Ah," he said, "them licks felt wonderful." He just couldn't wait to mix it up with those short, violent boys in the black pj's.

Twice in the next month, he was in the stockade, the first time for suggesting, in the middle of some sharp stick Mickey Mouse on the AT-56 grenade launcher, that good-hearted Uncle Sam (he of the brave, mighty and foursquare!) ought to give every fucking one of us a major-league a-tomic device with which we could incinerate not only our crafty enemy but also the leaf-mulch, rot and bug filth he hid among. "Doyle Wingo says ace those dudes!" He was standing on the top row of the field bleachers, yelling down at Sgt. Pike. "No more nickel and dime," he was hollering, "it's a time for bucks, gentlemen!" Pike had a twinkle in his eye that said all you needed to know about contempt and acceptable Army life. "Doyle says abandon all them plans and lay on the bravo thing he's talking about."

I told him to sit down, shut up, that Pike was going to nail his butt.

"Can't happen," he said, "this boy's got to live forever."

Next time he went to the stockade, it was for an impropriety with a PX clerk, a St. Francis High School teenager with action and cartilage enough to be called marvelous. He took it to her, he said, hopped over the watches and business machines counter, pinned her against the register, and licked her from chin to cheek, swirling her earlobes and nipping her nape. "She had the look," he told me later; "makes you want to grab hold," he said. "Brings out the best in a fellow." She had allowed him to feel the light and warmth of something, he said. Made him forget the fodder and runtlike nature of himself. She tasted swell, he said, like his girlfriend Betty Lou Bates, a beloved with Jayne Mansfield humpers and no shame. "Jesus," he sighed. "What a treat."

I could see it already: he'd either make a smoking hole in the ground or be the kind of meat-mess you'd need tongs and self-discipline to deal with. I told him, too. What with his attitude, I said, he was sure to step in It, be foolish enough to walk under It when It dropped from above, flush It from a hidey-hole or embrace It from loneliness—It being (Sgt. Pike said) that disturbed state of mind one experiences when the flesh rips or the head takes a beating from the whomp-splat of a projectile traveling at a wicked velocity. I told him to watch his step, remain vigilant, keep his weapon in order and mind his p's and q's because nine thousand miles from now we were just going to be two more bozos in an endeavor that specialized in blunder and scandal.

"O. T.," he said, "you haven't been listening, have you? Doyle Wingo is blessed."

The only time I saw Ears lose his composure was in an exercise Pike called Hit and Flee. I was Red Team and Ears Blue, ours an enterprise (Doyle said) in smashing, pounding, diverting, and employing the essential elements of creepy-crawly in the service of Winning. It wasn't much, really, just shag-assing through the desert at night, a klick this-away, a klick that, your face a spectacle of night-fighter cosmetic and purpose, your fondest friends a nature of grit, sticky bushes and night-sounds to be wary of. Around two hundred hours, I saw Ears in the inferior shelter of a mesquite tree, taking a leak.

O. T., I said to myself, school is in. Time to teach Wingo, Doyle E., a lesson.

I scooted into a dry arroyo, my heart thumping with anticipation. I had a fine view and when I made those two alien noises—both, I know now, the signal doom makes when it impends—I saw Doyle leap and collapse, a modern picture of arm and leg distress. "Shit," he was saying. "God-damn. God-damn." Later, I learned he'd dived into a cactus, taking several needles in the male parts. It was vintage *Action Comics:* dither and flight and scramble. By the moonlight, you could see his face—no camouflage, merely an oily sheen of shock with joyless eyeballs popping out.

"You were scared," I told him afterwards.

He was not, he said. What I'd seen on Doyle Wingo's face, he declared, was watchfulness and alarm, in addition to the play and wrinkle of a thought being translated into action. But not fear. Fear was for pantywaists. Wimps. Sure, Mr. Wingo maybe had an ache or something, a twitch, perhaps that jitter and heart-flop common to excitement, but not fright; no, not the sort of drool and blubber and pastiness old O. T. was describing.

"Ain't that the truth, O. T.?" he said. "It's the way Doyle says, right?"

"Ears," I said, "why are you here?"

"Choice," he said. Even in the dark, you could see his eyes were full of Christmas-like lights, happy and various. It was a pick, he confessed. Between, as the Honorable Judge Clarence P. Sanders put it, a long stay in the La Tuna federal calaboose or a shorter one aboard General Westmoreland's fighting machine. "My momma Tarvez said go, my daddy said go, even Betty Lou Bates said go. I went."

I have since told Audrey Jean that it was at this moment I discovered I truly liked Private Doyle Eugene Wingo. Though he was noise and bluster and I the insinuating sort, I felt we were buddies, an improbable pair; one a dingleberry, the other a would-be smoothie. "Did you tell him?" she asked once, implying that I should. "I did not," I said. Which was a continuing embarrassment. "Did he say anything?" she said. Yup, I said. He wondered what choice I had made. "None," I told him. It was a combination of bad fortune, three semesters of TCU failure, and a 6' 4" daddy who believed in patriotism as one of life's better works.

As it happened, months later Doyle and I ended up at the Do Long Bridge, in MR 2, just two among hundreds doing a shuffle called Survival in a place called Hardship. To be true, we were among those that Congressman Willard "Red" Sorrel (D-Mississippi) called "junkies, misfits and your basic criminal types." It was Ears the Congressman meant. Representative Sorrel flew in with a bunch of MACV kings and princes, humans used to sheets and cooked beef. First thing they saw was Doyle, shirtless in the LZ, wearing Dr. Jekyll surfer underpants and affecting the disposition of a man you might otherwise suspect as loco.

"I like to crush 'em," Doyle said. "Your man Wingo prefers to squash, bust up, dump doody on 'em."

You could see Mr. Sorrel was concerned. In a place of witlessness and direness that encouraged frank talk, all the civilization vanished right out of his face.

"Your Honor," Doyle said, grabbing our visitor by the knees, "do these folks a favor, will you?" Sorrel was nodding, nervously, the brass around him looking for local assistance. "Tell Captain Baird to turn this boy loose, okay? It needs to be done, and Doyle Eugene Wingo is the dude to do it."

In two days, my pal was gone.

"Where?" my wife asked once.

Nobody knew, I said. One story suggested that he'd inhaled X-4 vapors meant for the evil other guy and had been medivacked down to Hue City. Another said he'd joined the LURPs, recon gentlemen famous for shucking this mantle of vanquishments for the murder of the next. Rocky Perteet mentioned he'd seen Doyle on a contraband moped, said they'd been smoking that thick Laotian weed, said Doyle had employed the words *appointment* and *destiny*. He was mistaken, of course. I told Audrey Jean that surely Doyle was dead—if not dead in the bush somewhere, then soon to be dead in a cheap bar, or a short-shrift ambush, or pierced through by one of those celebrated stakes I never saw, or exploded in a duece-and-a-half, or stupid enough to cuddle next to jeopardy and its cruel companion grief.

A while later, I also was gone, the victim of an indiscretion in the heat of You-Know-What, having taken a piece of Mr. Minh's metal in the rear end. "O. T.," I said to myself, "put the best face on this incident. You're going home."

In the hospital in Tokyo, I received a couple of letters, one from Rocky Perteet.

"Let's me and you get together when this is over," he wrote. "We could go to California, do the beach trip."

I wrote him, no, thank you. I was putting this behind me. My character had been fully shaped, and I was now turning toward the future, my arms open to the goodies of the Great Whatever. I said sorry, don't look me up as I was going a thousand distances from that place—Alaska, maybe—a place as far from the present swelter as the good Mister Wingo was from life itself. I said that from now on, my adventures would be small, surely domestic, many involving children and delicate companions. I said bye-bye to the humid, the wanton, the random, and that sound the muscles make in the more hormonal moments of menace.

Bye-bye moil, I wrote. Bye-bye.

Which is how I viewed things until nearly a week ago when my daddy called, saying for me to bring Audrey Jean, the twins (Bonnie and Connie) and myself down from Michigan for a vacation, particularly now that my little sister Lee Ann was in the Miss New Mexico Universe pageant. "I'll pay," he said. "We'll play some golf, you like that. It's an occasion, boy. You ought to see Lee Ann, she's got breasts and everything."

That was fine, I said.

"Mother's got a new car, too," he said. "We'll break it in, what do you say?"

I like to think that it was at this instant I felt that spirit you hear so much about moving in me—that abstract and smoky doodah which is supposed to tote you into a fresh stage of understanding. But I also believe that I am reading too much into these events, such reading being the product of considerable wonder and much afterthought. In any case, I said sure, not knowing that I would be brought to the verge of seeing Doyle E. Wingo again. I should've guessed.

That first weekend down, we went to the Country Club— seedier than I remembered—my daddy and I in a foursome that included the club pro Ivy Martin and J. Benson Newell, recently of State Farm. I was the worst among them, a study of flail and thrash, my swing more pitiful than bad. I imagined people on the adjacent holes, scratching their necks in puzzlement, saying, "Is that man in pain or what?" I saw me as they might: a skinny male in a K-Mart sport shirt, lashing, sod and mud flying in a shower, the ball dribbling away. I felt good, though—uplifted, if you will—at home in the simple elements of sunshine, bent Bermuda and personable partners. One time, at the eighth hole, my daddy hanging over a sizable putt, his face as innocent as a bird's, his arms a mottle of moth patches and sunburn, I said, "Hold it."

My ancient father looked at me like I was naked.

"Daddy," I said, "I love your ass, you know?"

He shook his head mournfully. "O. T. shut up and let me putt, will you?"

Then I heard a noise which put my heart in my ears and a grunting sound—uh, uh, uh—in my brain.

"Your shot," Daddy said. We were playing for the championship of the Western World. Plus a two-dollar skins game.

"Mister Martin," I said, "who's that?" I was pointing at a man in a green Day-Glo outfit on the next fairway. It was a figure of interest, all right—the kind of being thrown up, I know now, by turmoil, its finer touches finished by the rearward features of our nature.

"Don't know," Ivy Martin said. The club, he complained,

was letting almost anybody in now—Arab, Wop, woman with one tooth. "I expect to see a monkey out here one day. Shit, I expect to sell that hairy animal a wedge if I can."

In the other fairway, near a sand trap, that figure was hopping and hooting, around him a woman and a pair of youngsters. You could hear him plainly: "Aaarrrgghhh! Uuummmppphhh!"

"Make that putt, boy," my daddy was saying. "Next hole, we'll get us a beer."

We followed that man and his family the rest of the afternoon, me drifting into a distracted state akin to confusion. There was addle in my thoughts. A kind of melancholy, too. I felt orphaned—castaway, adrift, exiled. It was Doyle Wingo, I was sure. The walk was the slope-shouldered lurch I remembered, the curious head-cock as familiar to me as my own hand. One time, I watched him tee off on a par three, the ball making that thwock-pock of authority. I saw him study its flight, then throw up his arms in manful joy and sweep up that woman who was tending his bag. Lord, it was a moment freighted with desire and its perfected object. Betty Lou Bates. You could see she was svelte—not limp or wasted at all—and for an instant I felt as if it were I who was being caught up and swung with such glee. It was a scene that wanted only tears, the sweet music of Henry Mancini and a long time to recover.

"What's wrong with you, O. T.?" Mr. Newell said. "Next time, don't drink from the bottle. You get too much air."

"Perk up, son," my daddy said. "Today's our lucky day."

Two holes later, I was almost close enough to Wingo to see expression. Yup, I was saying to myself. Yup. Yup. My heart was banging in its spot like a fish in a tub; and it took me a moment to identify this thump-whack as fear—that clammy and close emotion you experience when those famous veils drop away and there ain't nothing between you and certainty but light and distance. He was wearing a Hubie Green hat, but I believed I could see enough of his eyes, even in shadow, to know that he'd glimpsed death several times, escaped it always by a nick and felt special enough to taunt it from any of the available havens. He was talking now, bent over his ball, his kids and lady a dozen paces aside, his lip action—as I knew it would be—still furious, his words doubtlessly addressing important acts and themes. O. T., I told myself, you do not want to go over there. Ever.

"Daddy," I announced, "if you don't mind, I'll pick up here." What with the handicaps, we were winning by four anyway. "I'll see you at home."

That night, as I am telling you now, I told Audrey Jean the whole story, leaving off the filigree I might yet use if I get a dotage. In my old room, in my twin beds, the cowboy curtains of my youth stirring in our desert breezes, I told her about the golfing and the light and my shivering and Doyle Eugene Wingo swaggering about, his presence full of a hero's energy that puts all else in a dark spot.

"Audrey Jean," I whispered, "I'm a fine person, right?"

The light was like silver in that room, several of her body parts points of gleam and shine. She said I had my virtues: sense of humor, respectfulness, manners useful enough for company, interests in topics like mechanics, good health, and a demeanor that was often superior. I could hear my momma and daddy watching Johnny Carson in their room, plus the telltale sleep-creaks my twins were making in theirs.

"I'm glad he didn't die," I said. "Truly."

"Are you crying, O. T.?"

I told her—and it was the truth—that I was not; rather, I was overcome, the symptoms being a tightness beneath the sternum like a vise over the heart and an extravagant riot in the crimped medulla: I was seeing again, from my spot in the pro shop, Doyle and his family climb into an auto so high and clumsy and chrome-covered it seemed from another era. I was seeing the hair and teeth and spindly legs of that which had passed through the hurt and come out a beautiful and masterful thing.

"C'mere," I said to Audrey Jean and, thankfully, she did, all her moistness and breath and frilly nightwear transporting me, I see it now, to that rare place Doyle had been all along; that place, free of threat and worry, where, in the company of pride and ignorance, we could live handsome and free and forever.

THE PURPOSE OF THIS CREATURE MAN

I recognized him straight away, from the picture in his autobiography *Hands Up!*

"I ain't afraid of you," I declared, having intercepted him
on the wood sidewalk, the rain washing off his brushed fedora in waves. I was fourteen, I told him, possibly rash but
completely educated at the Newata (OK) School of Industrial Arts where I excelled in gymnasium and sums. "I am
passing scared of mange and toothy beasts and losing my
way, but *you*—I ain't frightened of your bulk nor cheerless
eyes."

"Of course, you're not," he told me. "You're the cheap
sort. To you, life's shortness is its virtue." He had a gleaming, sawed-off Winchester scattergun he wore in a shoulder
holster. It was glamorous and, tucked away like that under
his armpit, truly unique and modern. "Me," he was saying,
"I prefer length and vice. Excuse me."

Friends, Doc Leroy Toolchin, like desperadoes everywhere, was gifted and beautiful, as removed from ordinari-
ness as God; you could see the wonder and specialness in his
eyes that rain-besieged afternoon he parked his 1906 Hobbes
motorcar in the mud outside the Palace Post Office. (Palace
didn't have a bank then, just a Washington & St. Louis
Dial-Lock Drop Steel Safety Box and a consumptive clerk
to tend it.) Doc was alone, and his face said, *Citizens, be still.
My profession is violent but I will be gone shortly.*

"Money is pain," he told the decent folks inside. "Hands
up."

At the door, I saw him stroll among them like T. Roose-
velt, saying *how-do* and *good mornin'* and *fear not, I am
indeed cutthroat but likewise patient.* Oh, it was a splendid
ten minutes. The Doc, in a tuneful speech, addressed himself
to the contemporary themes of thrift and sacrifice, while that
clerk—Mr. DeHenry was his name—nervously fiddled with
the safety box.

"I am a graduate of the Stillman Academy of Chiropractic
Medicine of Peoria, Illinois," he announced. "I can cure
sciatica, the bloody flux, swallowed air, shooting pains and
greater dissatisfactions, like Disappointment and Coldheart-
edness."

I was thrilled, my heart in my neck like a squirrel, all claws
and climbing. The Doc was legendary in these parts of
Oklahoma, and I had no larger hope than to be him or one
of his blessed firebrands.

"You there!" The Doc was addressing a civilian who looked
hangdog and sullen. "Exercise. Avoid melancholy. Read of
misfortune bushwhacked by gumption."

To another, a youth like myself, bug-eyed and overawed:

"Son, think of me as an unwelcome but polite relative. In the meantime, stand upright and square. Posture's lifelong and chronic."

To a third: "You're shiftless, I can tell. Flee the lowlife; join the Army. Be erect in all things."

Up close, you could see in his shining, bardlike face shaving nicks and itinerant hairs. His was a life, I had read, of *deprivation overcome by wit, love undone by need.* He'd been a fat man once, but was now lean as a result of self-discipline and an eye for finer things. Plus, he had teeth like a Knabe piano.

"Mr. DeHenry," he said at last, "I would appreciate it if you hurry, thank you."

In an instant, he was again standing beside me, more out the door than in, rain rattling the rotted eaves above, saying adios and good health. "You have been stuck up by a master," he said. "In the future, accept no less." His odors were pungent—not sweats, I know now, but the warm, close fragrances of Grue, Wist and Human Longing.

Then, he was gone, richer and tooting his Gabriel exhaust horn bye-bye, me standing with the amused and outraged, watching him disappear like a ghost.

"You'll see more of me!" I shouted after him. "I'll be in your face one day. You wake up, it'll be me there—me and probably the gang that worships me. I won't be rude to you; I'll be generous!"

I, the veteran of two cheap but daring armed robberies in Missouri, saw the Doc again in four months. He was traveling with two Mexicans, lonesome and ignorant sorts, each with a face like an unwholesome thought, outlaws on account of deficiencies of spirit not calling.

We ran into each other after a meeting of the No Treaty Party in Tulsa, him wheeling his Hobbes through the thick evening dust, his two loyal bad guys trotting behind on horseback.

"We could be partners," I told him.

"What's your name?"

I told him I was semi-French, with some Negro and Creek mixed in. "La Duc," I said. He could call me Mister in keeping with my aspirations and fancy manners.

"I already have associates," he said, now puffing a stubby, rank Egyptian Deity. "These gentlemen are without ambitions. Plus, they're desperate."

I was smart, I told him. My virtues: Keenness, Youth, a Stealthful Demeanor and Curiosity. "I can climb, run, peep through curtains, drop from a reasonable height to the back of a well-trained horse, make drink from such grasses and weeds as rush pink and swamp potato. I can imitate specific fowl, crawl easily in spooky places, and make a host of machine noises by way of diversion." I could be invaluable, I said, as precious to him as gold and good health.

"I think not," he said, starting his motorcar. "See me again when you've aged and learned fear."

Doc was waiting for me when I got out of the Ohio State Penitentiary in Columbus. I had lived with the glorious O. Henry and had learned certain but minor truths and a feel for art's fineness, but not fear. "Life looks backwards," Mr. O. Henry had once told me. "What has happened is divine and planned." He had been a caballero in Honduras and knew, I thought, whereof he spoke; but he was only the second most famous person I knew and, compared to the

Doc, not a jot more notorious than yesterday's celebrated sleepyhead or kidnapped baby.

"I am putting together a gang of outlaws," Doc said. We were meeting at Knocker's, an Oaks saloon, me in a shiny prison suit like something from Karno's Wow Wows, the Doc magnificent in a silk vest and morning coat. His was a figure of excellence and tasteful grooming. "I'm looking for venal men," he said. "I place a premium on the nefarious, the ne'er-do-well. You'll do nicely."

"Why would I want to join?" I said. I was still hurt, the way he brushed me off three years ago. Besides, I told him, I was thinking about organizing a gang, too. "I understand Wobblies are aggressive," I said. "Orphans, too. Like me. Anyway, you're prissy."

"You couldn't organize a sit-down dinner." he said. "You've got to have a reputation. A vision helps. Plus, I've a name for you. It's Duke."

I preferred Ringo.

"Duke's got elegance," he said. "It says boldness. It says dashing."

"What's Ringo say?"

He thought for a time, eyes on the skies. "It says, 'Help me, please. I am lost and need finding.' "

Doc was right.

"You'll be number two in my outfit. Think of me as your daddy or first friend on earth." He wanted boys on the edge of things, he said, a new issue of bad guy for the new and bad times ahead.

"Why me?" I said. "I wasn't spit to you before."

His face got sly, like a fresh development in thought.

"I like your enthusiasm," he said. "In addition, you're strong, which is an advantage in toting away the booty."

Outside there were knotty little trees and a sky like a cheap birthstone, a picture as meager as my imagined future. Doc was right: I had nothing but vigor and a need to please. "Okay," I said. "I reckon I can be a help to you."

In three days we were over in Eureka Springs, taking the healing baths, the word of our enterprise having spread among the area's gunmen and banditos. Oklahoma was a state then, but still a haven for riffraff and brigands.

The first to appear was Chicken Jim.

"Listen to me," Doc whispered in my ear. "You're about to learn how to separate the lofty from the hindmost."

"I am aroused by danger," Jim was saying. His posture was all eyeballs and elbows, his hair original and naughty. "In a fight, I am madness itself."

"What kind of God you believe in?" Doc said. "Morbid or wrathful?"

"Both," Chicken Jim answered, shivering with anticipation. "My God's fully evolved. I look upon Him as stern and fugitive." Trainer, Councillor, crafty Guide—his Lord was havoc and weal, both. "I'm experienced," Jim said. He'd ridden with the Hardwick boys in Tarrant County, robbed only the deserving, left the no-account to battle the baleful themselves. "I can cook, know a couple of novel tunes, and shoot. Mainly shoot." Here, his face antic with pride, he fired three rounds into the wall above us. The Doc didn't flinch. "I'm a shootist with taste."

"You're in," Doc said, flicking some debris off his shoulder.

Then, to me: "Outlawry, like the physical and humanistic sciences, is a special calling. Odd is good, Duke. Were he here, I would take Darwin and his monkey companion."

This is how we talked in those days: directly and as if life depended on it.

After Chicken Jim came Big Bob Cook, a short and intemperate hombre who would be hung by Judge Parker in Ft. Smith within two years.

"My specialty's advanced understanding," he told us. "Look at my face; it's heavy with learning."

He looked hungry to me.

"You want to know something about Affection, noxious vapors, or them tiny paths of circulations for your bloods and wastes, then I'm your man."

Doc lit a cigarette, his expression contemplative. "I bet you're shrewd, right?"

"I know quotes from Utillo and Sange, how to eat cowbird, a little about the planets, namely Mars. Presently, I am extending thoughts into Kings and Queens." His face was red with excitement. "Take me on, Doc. Otherwise, I'll drift."

"I appreciate a man with feeling," Doc said. "Welcome aboard."

For two weeks, we occupied rooms upstairs at the Dorsett, conducting interviews, the Doc a canny judge of character. To a Chinaman named Foo, known thereabouts as a smiling and cool killer, the Doc said, "You're out. I shun the obtuse and nostalgic. I suggest you get your own outfit. Go to Texas. Death's a pleasure there." He turned away the weepy, the woebegone and the mournful, saying the membership in his gang required grit and steadfastness. "I want the massive, love-loose and wicked," he said one night. "In this world, there's little room for the merely mad or those with low needs."

I turned away plenty, too—mainly the handicapped, those

well wracked by misfortune. "Go into real estate, hunt for oil," I told one gent who had rheumy eyes and a disturbing, intestinal cough. "Doc's gang is touched and wondrous. You would do well in conventional work." He went off gratified.

In the third week, an Idaho cowboy drifted in. He called himself Perceval, said he was a poet. "I cleave to the romantic and dreadful," he told us. "My verse is deadly."

The Doc was impressed. Words redeem, he said, and give the heart something to beat for.

"Death is all around," Perceval was saying. "I aim to endure." He recited one—a sonnet, I believe—whose themes were grief and the worn path to bliss. "I can do this in Spanish or German," he said. "Languages improve the mind."

"You're in," Doc said. "The subtle has a place in our world."

The last we accepted was the Verdigris Kid, no favorite of mine. He was a sissy, called everybody Darling and Sweet Chips, and wore a woman's kidney-heel shoes.

"You like boys, right?" I said.

"I like innocence." His eyelids fluttered like a coquette or apprenticed bar-girl. "I prefer the hairless and narrow-chested. Manhood's a bore, darling. Give me the smells and sensitive skin of youngsters."

"What do you do with them?" I asked.

"The usual," he said, "hugging, squeezing. I'm bred for the gentle half of heaven."

I was against him.

"What's in prison?" Doc said to me.

It was an easy question. In prison, I said, were horse thieves, back-stabbers, dry-gulchers, claim-jumpers, those who were daft or nearly so, robbers like ourselves, runaways from such as Kettle Hill, drunk Indians, waylayers, and those with base appetites.

"Wrong," Doc said. "In prison are males. The Kid makes the time pass with his loving. You ought to be ashamed."

I looked at the Kid. He had shoulder-length curls and Cupid's pouty lips. His smile suggested a rich inner life. I remembered seeing him one time in an English party gown and a comb with paste pearls.

"What's your specialty?" I said.

"Sweet-talking," he said. "I can get you in and out with a word. In addition, I can impersonate. Listen to my voice." He sang something from the Orpheum Variety Spectacle, then did a speech that mentioned age and youth and the difference between them.

"All right," I said. "We're open-minded."

Our first job was the White Bros. Savings Bank in Fayetteville, Arkansas. Big Bob Cook charged in first. "I have read Mr. Freud and know my desires to be prehistoric smuts," he shouted. "Hands Up!"

The dozen folks in there turned white with fear, one lady fainting into Doc's arms, her skirts rustling above her dimpled knees. Gently, he set her on the floor, rubbing her wrists and blowing across her feverish forehead with breath, she later told the *Monitor,* as sweet as autumn and wax.

Perceval hit the tellers' cages, robbing each with a smile and a new literary discovery. "Look into my eyes," he told one man, "what do you see?" The man was trembling, picking unconsciously at his shirtfront: "Evil?"

"Nope," Perceval cried, "I am ascetic and hollow. Irony is what I am, your last chance to be immortal."

I took the vault while Chicken Jim picked the pockets of these upright and easily panicked strangers. "Believe me," he told the manager, a squatty fellow with Bull Moose moustaches, "death does not especially hurt. You got to take the long view in these things. Think of your Redeemer, up there looking down. He's got a happy reward for you."

In fifteen minutes we scrambled out of there, the Kid having stolen a beaded reticule and a pointy parasol.

"If God hadn't wanted them sheared," Doc was hollering over the clang and bang of his motorcar as we hightailed from town, "He wouldn't have called them sheep."

The next eight months were joyful. We hit the substantial communities of southern Missouri and western Kansas, marching into their banks and post offices and mercantile stores without remorse or difficulty. "Big Bob," Perceval said one night, "tell me your words at Liberty; this is for our book."

His face lit with pride, Big Bob said his words had been— what?—*lambent* and *fulminous*. "I saw myself as Locke and Milton or deep-thinking Euclid," he said, "men dealing in dangerous but everlasting thought."

Perceval was writing to newspapers, broadcasting our fame and special personalities. *Thus far,* he wrote in an article for the *Daily Headlight* in Sapulpa, *we have not killed or injured. We rely on intimidation and the victim's good sense.* To be true, we hadn't got much, hundreds not thousands of dollars at each place. Perceval wrote of us that we were valiant true-bloods, surprising and, like the end of a good story, inevitable. My nineteenth birthday we boarded the old Iron-Pacific. Only Big Bob Cook had his weapon out.

"Answer my questions and live," he told the baggage clerk.

The man squirmed and bit his lips.

"What comes before Duty and Employment?"

"I-I-I-I-I," the man blubbered, his tiny hand quivering in the air.

"We come before all," Big Bob declared. "Trust me, we're clean inside, all loved by somebody. We had mothers, too."

Doc stood in front of the safety box, his face a puzzle. "Pray for us, Jim."

"In light and in pain—" Chicken Jim began, moiling over the box like a heedless lover, addressing the Lord in His wisdom to set aside the ordinary and human and reveal, without mystery *please,* how to open that infernal safe.

"Know what kind of hole this'll make?" The Kid had his pistol stuck in the clerk's dainty ear.

"What's your name?" Doc said.

"B-B-Burt." It came out as a choked whisper.

"Well, Burt," Doc said, "know how many meals and fine times you will miss if you die now? Think of women, too—I assume you're normal. Think of sentiment and happy moments sure to come. We're optimists, all of us. We subscribe to the better life. What do you subscribe to?"

With pleasure, he told us the combination. It developed he subscribed to, among other things, living long. Relief and intelligence came to his face when he knew he would live, and we left him smiling, saying adieu.

We were hot after that. Every marshal was trailing us, even the special Indian Deputies from the Nations. The Verdigris Kid was for splitting up, going separate and alone into, say, New Mexico, himself disguised as either Louise Fazenda or a Mack Sennett heroine.

"I am for hiding," I said. "We could lay low, come up even more glorious a year from now."

Perceval was without opinion. "I am in this for experience," he said, "and seasoning."

Through it all, Doc said little. He stood at the stove, frying cheese steaks and stirring beans, his lovely, pure face glazed with steam. At that minute I knew I loved him—not like the Kid, unwisely and unnaturally—but as a brother or pop or revered school teacher. I loved him because he'd saved me from being ordinary or unimportant as range dust. Outside it was freezing, our woolly and footsore horses pulled inside the only outbuilding with Doc's new Packard; but inside— here in this Creek Nation shotgun cabin of rough pine boards and uneven floors—the Doc warmed us all, even that remote and beauty-soaked Perceval. We could stay months, I was thinking. "The century is young," learned Bob Cook said, greedily shoveling away his meal. "Let's cogitate and carry on with our inventive ways."

In the morning, they hit us—having learned our whereabouts, the story went, with the aid of divination and sneakiness. At first, I thought it was Chicken Jim's righteous but vicious dreams, a series of lesser devils and torments floating up from the dark waters of his sleep; but, as I lay in my longjohns, coiled in my blankets, I could hear whispering and, at last, a shower of pebbles against the hammered tin roof.

The Doc, nimble and gleeful, sprang from his cot. "I was dreaming about today," he told me. The half-light of dawn was eerie, the fog and early mists yet to lift from the canebreaks and dwarf pines. "I was thinking how I'd die."

We were a maze of movement, deliberate and quick.

"Doc," Big Bob said, "they're moving your motorcar."

Through the smudged windows, you could see a handful of men pushing the Packard out of the shed and into the treeline. I was tracking one of them with my Navy Blue Colt. He was the Chinaman Doc had turned away two years ago.

"It's the lure of money," Doc said, noting my surprise. "That and a close brush with mortality. I applaud Mr. Foo's good sense."

"Please," Percevel said, leveling his rifle. "Look at that smile; he could die happy."

"Not yet." The Doc looked abstract and distant. "I had a vision. It was a morning such as this. They were who they are: mean and shortsighted, swept onto the law's side by liquor and the safety of numbers."

"And we?" I said.

Doc's face was a blaze of rue. "I'm sorry to say, Duke, we did not all survive."

The smells and sounds are what I remember in this year, 1947. Chicken Jim hung at my back, his breath rough, muttering about Judgment and Fore-ordination and The Purpose of This Creature Man. I believed I could hear his heart pounding with rage against this unhappy turn of events. He said heaven was a place of light love, soulful and satisfying. Eats were plenty; obligations few. Hombres like us—excluding the Kid, perhaps—would dwell in the untroubled hereafter, bathe in eternal waters. It was uplifting and a true comfort.

With Doc, at the other window, were the others, the Kid's face still sleep-creased, not at all lovely. "One of those boys is pretty," he was saying. "To slay him will be a shame." Jim, as usual, was aroused by his closeness to death. Noisily, he pulled his boots on and laced himself into his custom leather vest, thick enough (the story went) to protect against all but point-blank shots. Perceval's face was scarlet. You could see he was transported. "Doc," he was saying. "tell me what you're thinking. This is for posterity!"

Bob Cook looked smug. "I have taken shelter in the perdurable insights of Bentham and Ben Franklin," he said, "Bring on the gunplay!"

"Doc!" a fellow outside called, "put on your trousers and come out. Let's parley."

I was for it, I told Doc. I quoted a fair amount of his book, namely the parts about valor, discretion, and the species' need to live forever.

"I know you," Doc hollered out. "You're Sweet Water Charley Bascom."

The man's smile was a carnival of pride.

"What have you done with my motorcar?"

Sweet Water Charley Bascom pointed. In a stand of trees, a dozen lawmen and citizens had scrambled atop the Packard like gibbons. "It was ill-gotten," he said. "We have confiscated it."

"Charley," Doc said. His tone told you his motives were complex. "Have you ever been to the sea?"

"Once." Charley said he'd been to New Orleans three years ago where he lay on the beach, smoking Murad cigarettes, and absorbed the healthful sunshine. "I ate shrimps, slept in an eighty-dollar bed, and had my picture taken by a fellow named Bellocq. Initials E. J."

"Who went with you?" Doc said.

For a second, Sweet Water Charley looked confused. "My wife, why?"

"Think of her now," Doc said sorrowfully. "Visualize her welcome thighs and that good heart which renews."

Understanding reached him before the bullets.

"Whaaa—?" he said as Perceval's blast toppled him. He took it in the belly, doubling over and falling forward, landing with a splash in a well-puddle. Those aboard the Packard stiffened with surprise then dived for cover, a flurry of buckskins and three-dollar hats.

"Boys," Doc said to us, "never tell a man you stole the thing he loves."

The battle—not at all the good-natured shoot-'em-up you see in the movies nowadays—took about an hour. Big Bob Cook was the first to get plugged. "I have a higher brain," he'd told us, throwing open the door. "Watch me outwit these farmers." He went, perhaps, eight steps before the foolishness hit him. That slug must have thrown him ten feet. "Damn," he was crying, seriously wounded and lying in the weeds.

Now, I can admit I was scared, short of breath and tense, jerking without purpose, aiming here and there, my heart pounding like a drop forge. The Kid was shrieking, his face alive with queer horror. Even Perceval seemed touched by the impending doom. "Duke," he hollered while he reloaded, "preserve my memory. Here are my verses." He thrust on me a notebook full of pith and poems scrawled close to the margins—all, I discovered later, virtually wanton with hope. A second later, a round nipped him in the shoulder and he passed out, eyelids fluttering. Bullets were slamming into the walls, a few ringing off the stove.

The Doc said, "Hold it."

The Kid's face was inflamed and tear-stained, his hair a distraught mess. Outside, Big Bob Cook lay moaning—"What's the use of principle and vast knowledge against the hard feelings of a hundred lawmen!"—one leg twitching, the other working as if he were upright and running headlong toward life. Beside me, Chicken Jim had soiled himself in the excitement. All the holiness was out of his eyes.

"We are in an extreme moment here, boys," Doc said. "Who's for giving up?"

Slowly, my hand was raised. "Sorry," I said. "I can think of better places to die."

"Me, too," Chicken Jim said. "I'm thirty-one; Jesus and them eternal waters can wait."

"What about you, Kid?" Doc's face was dark. "I suppose you're looking forward to close confinement and a captive audience."

The Kid nodded, smiled. "I can be comfortable any-where," he said. "We sissies are a flexible kind."

Doc was abashed, but, perhaps out of sympathy for us lesser types, he didn't scold, just slid down the wall and sat slumped, that scattergun across his ample lap like a tired but living animal. "I did my first robbing at nineteen," he said. "I stole less than fifty dollars and gave it all the next night to a woman named Ruby. I was a sophomore at the Stillman Academy and had learned anatomy by then—the heart-bones and tough muscles and fragile nerves. I was a student of manipulation, of certain bodily centers of grief. But it was outlawry which gratified." It made, he said, his flesh and gray thought-cells come alive. It was peril which cured flatulence and fatigue; peril, not bending and popping and hearty squeezing.

He was quiet for a second, then whispered, "Go on, I will see you presently."

They starved him out. They denied him comfort, useful

conversation with his peers—the thousand things which invigorate and sustain. For a week—Percevel, Chicken Jim, the Verdigris Kid and I hogtied to separate trees—that posse waited, all of them cautious and thankful. They ate noisily, some sang, the inquisitive from close-by appeared, and they remained patient, watchful, somber and earnest. Then, Doc came out, numb and weak-kneed from lack of rest, and they surrounded him, their faces sullen and shameful; within months, we were in distant hoosegows, Big Bob Cook mistakenly hung for the murder of Sweet Water Charley Bascom.

I was in the Tahlequah Penitentiary for five years, released in August 1916, then twenty-four years old but still a baby inside, innocent and dumb. I had written Doc once, saying, *I am fine in spirit and in body, though often fatigued. There is a society here, of which I am the Treasurer, the Friendly Sons of Elmer Rice. Conditions here are dire but recreation is permitted. Baseball is a favorite and competition fierce. I think of you regularly and with pride. Think of me, too.* Now, three decades removed from the actions I am describing, I see why he did not reply; he must have seen me as I was, foolhardy and stubborn, moving without understanding in a world modern and weary and tragic.

Doc surprised me in Tulsa. I was employed at an Express Station, guard and ofttimes errand-boy—humiliating but gainful. It was afternoon and I did not recognize him at first, his body soft and fat. I was sweeping and he caught my elbow, saying, "I have another job in mind."

I felt I had been touched by the fingers of the past and they lay against my heart with affection and true regard. "Where?"

His eyes glittered. "In Texas." There was a Punitive Expedition into Mexico, he said, going after Pancho Villa. "There's ten thousand soldiers, every one of whom is regularly if not well paid." We would strike in El Paso, the paymaster's office at Ft. Bliss, pickings easy and sure and plenty. "I've spoken to the others," he said, "they will join us in time."

"I missed you," I said.

"We'll use disguise this time." His breath was an odor that put one in mind of the future, its joy and peace. "We'll be ranchers, wealthy and such. I've got to think on it."

"I studied your book," I told him. I could tell different chapters by only feeling the warp in the page. More than a dozen paragraphs I knew by heart. What'd he want to hear from, I wondered. The episodes of might, such as those near Tinney, or those wherein wit proved a useful gift?

"What do you say, Tump?" All the age was out of his cheeks. "I can count on you, right?"

It was a moment of supreme expectancy, a tug at the wants and needs of me. I looked around. Even the light had weight and purpose.

"Okay," I said. "I wouldn't mind being wealthy again."

Chicken Jim joined up in September, in Odessa. He had put aside his usual God, having taken up (he said) with Beings too mordant and cruel to explain. "I was fury," he told us. "My keepers swore I was in touch with vipers and Satan's imagination. I ate little, feigned paralysis. They had to let me go."

Outside of Brownfield, rains beating down in torrents, we met the Kid, almost pure woman now. He was wearing a dress of French lace and lady's underclothes, his face clownish, mean.

"Jail was evil," he said. "I loved it."

In October, the air crisp and cool, Perceval stopped Doc Toolchin's Dodge touring car outside San Ysidro. He'd lost an ear.

"It is gone in the defense of the ideal," he explained. "No matter. I have fled poetry and its pansy ways. I am now an essayist. Let's ride."

Except for the clippy-clop of Perceval's shaggy horse and the steady putter of the Dodge, the last fifty were silent miles, contemplative and long, the land rugged and alien in the manner of storybook deserts everywhere. We'd all changed; and what had done it was neither time, nor rigor, nor indescribable hardship; what had changed us was being without Doc, his example and his presence. "Without Doc," C. J. would say later, "we were in a dark land, without direction or consumable spirits." It was a quote from Doc's book.

In silence, we took rooms on the third floor of the Cortez Hotel, closed the heavy curtains and in the almost airless dark slept a week in shifts, each of us furtive but eager. We got haircuts and baths at the Chinese Emporium on Stanton Street, two watching while two sat in that grim, gray water. *Duke,* I thought one night, *you are all but dead, these boys your smiling angels.* It was an insight Doc would've called cheap, but it held me as tightly as I am now held by time and these worn memories. It was in silence, too, that Doc arranged the details of our enterprise, coming into the rooms one afternoon and lifting from his valise his special sawed-off gun. "Gentlemen," he said. His voice should have been a thunderclap or the first bell of doom; but it was a sweet whisper that put a shiver in your bones: "Tomorrow we will be renewed and rid of these hard times."

■

That Friday we rolled through the entrance to Ft. Bliss in Doc's rattling Dodge, all of us outfitted in puttees, campaign hats and Sam Browne belts (courtesy of the Kid's guile and Perceval's skill with a club). Doc was a Colonel, much decorated and vain, the rest of us vulgar and from the serving-class.

"Be comforted, boys," Doc told us, as we went through the camp under iron-gray November skies. "We are an experienced and wise outfit."

Chicken Jim was inspired. "Last night," he said, "I made my peace. I told my Lord I was prepared and fearless. I said I could go out of this world without a tear. Know what he said?"

We didn't.

"Nothing." Jim's face was shining with faith. "He's close-mouthed, that's why I love Him."

At the paymaster's building, a whitewashed clapboard affair with windows covered by a latticework of bars and screens, we got out and went to our tasks as arranged, the Kid darting around back, his face as lifeless and pale as ash.

"Nobody move!" Perceval hollered as we burst in the door, hurling two sleepy guards to the floor. "As a gang, we are efficient and abstract about death," he declared, waving his pistol for emphasis. His hat, raggedy and well stained, was pulled low on his forehead so his eyes, covered in shadow, looked as impossibly poetic as stone. "As individuals, we are all sons-of-bitches. My advice: seek approval from us and be quiet. Thank you."

Quickly, I leaped over the tellers' cages and went through their money drawers, excitedly filling my large bag. Here I am, I was thinking, alive and once again secure in my place in this swell universe. It was a hopeful thought.

"I'm Toolchin," Doc was saying to a sergeant with fleshy, vein-splashed cheeks. "For you, I recommend exercise and self-restraint with food." To another, apparently the sergeant's helper, Doc prescribed Higher Thoughts. "Flee the recondite, young fella," he said. "Study deeds and how to master them. Also, pull your stomach in."

Chicken Jim, by the window as a lookout, was jubilant, mentioning (in order of importance) the mercies of God, among them fettle and feck. I felt charmed, as select and eternal as a star.

It was then the first shot was fired, and the Verdigris Kid dashed through the side-door.

"Darlings," our sissy said, "we have company."

In minutes, hundreds of troopers were assembled outside, a dozen Quad and Peerless trucks drawn up as barricades. The troopers all had faces like vigilance itself—grim and dark with outrage.

"What happened?" I said.

Angrily, Chicken Jim said it was Fate, Normal Mysteries and the Twentieth Century. "Time and place and circumstance have come together," he said. "We are about to be crushed." It was an upsetting picture he drew—one in which those such as me and mine were powerless, as significant to the order of things as flea, ugly bird or poor man's idea.

Perceval agreed. It was a life, he was saying, of suffering, inexact rewards and failure. "It's a wonder we're still alive. Look at those hombres!"

You could see those Army boys moving quickly, in places almost five deep in a ring around our building. They all looked like Jim's dream-devils—skinny, whey-faced and as compassionate as gunpowder.

"Fret not," the Kid said. "We have hostages."

For a second, that room was still as a mool. Even the six troopers lined up against a wall were frozen. You could see they were entertaining disturbing thoughts. I felt hot and dirty. Then my pinky finger started twitching.

"We should let these inside people go," I said. They were defenseless and proper-minded and probably not without virtue. It was unfair to kill them thus. We would be no more upright and worthy, say, than Arapaho Brown and other murderous copycats. "I ain't a back-stabber and a bully," I said.

"I don't care," Perceval said. "My book can do without this experience."

"Me," Chicken Jim was saying, "I've got a big heart; let 'em go."

"What say, Doc?" The Kid had his pistol in the gut of the sergeant. "They could be a hindrance or a great help."

At that instant, the troopers let loose with a horrendous volley. Doc's Dodge was shredded, bullets ripping into the upholstery, the radiators, the tires going flat, metal pinging and screeching, until that car sat steaming, the windscreen fractured, one riddled door swinging with a creak. I watched Doc's face the whole time, noting how his cheeks grew tense. A vein throbbed at his temple. It was as if the Doc himself had been battered.

"Right," he said at last, "a man would no more hide behind another than speak ugly to his momma or wish for the dark flames of hell." You could tell he was depressed. "Let them go."

Carefully, the Kid opened the door, waving a white hankie. "Here are your babies," he shouted. "Let's dance!"

For a time, we sat, quiet and still as wax figures, that room seeming to grow smaller and gloomier. I watched Doc, his long fingers with well-tended nails, wondering what I should do, what I should say. I felt alone and very young.

"What will you do tomorrow?" Chicken Jim said. "Me, I'm taking up the simple, useful pleasures. Perhaps farming."

Perceval said he'd had enough experience. "I intend to organize my thoughts, pull heartstrings. You will read about me in three years. My books will be popular and true."

It was silly, unrealistic talk—wishful thinking, at best. We were going nowhere, except to perdition—a place we would enter in pieces, an arm or a leg at a time, our bloods and faces last.

"What about you, Darling Doc?"

"Boys," he sighed, "I have cured palsy and weak knee-joints. I am now fifty-six years old and weary. Maybe, I'll retire. Get married. There's something to be said for lying in the arms of an understanding and thick-waisted woman." He went on for a few minutes, his eyes bright but remote, saying that he could be a consultant for industry. Maybe an agent for the Missouri Steam Washer Company. "I'm getting out of robbing, though," he said, nodding with conviction. "I've tried to be bigger than my times, boys. Instead of going the practiced and usual ways, I have been a celebrity. Now, I think I'll go back to being human."

"Me, too," I said. I was touched.

The afternoon wore on with negotiations, an Army Colonel urging moderation and horse sense. I was thinking of

Big Bob Cook; had he been there, and not a restive ghost luminous in the afterworld, he would have argued for more exploits and hugger-mugger. His would have been a plan full of frenzy, inspired if not practical.

The Kid was disinterested. 'I'm past approval or care," he said. "You're the ones I love."

Chicken Jim was steadfast: "Touch my skin," he said, "that's the cool of a man at home with the hereafter."

Then it came out of me, unplanned but honestly put: "Let's fight it out." I quoted that part from Doc's book about thine own self and hewing and pressing yourself forward when others were shrinking from the fray or fleeing in panic. I said: "What about that time in Rogers, Doc? You had a gang then, too. You told them to shoot, shoot, shoot. What else is there?"

"Right," Jim said. "We're desperadoes, ain't we?"

Perceval's eyes were wet. You could tell he was having an aesthetic thought.

"Okay, boys," Doc said, resting his scattergun on the sill. "You convinced me."

So we did. With considerable enthusiasm—the Kid's face a study of something approaching mirth, Chicken Jim yelling about a soiled flock and its generous shepherd, myself in high and happy animation, Perceval stripping himself naked but for a pair of artful underwear—we shot, Doc pointing and offering trenchant, if not timely, advice. "Know and love," he said once, "and win at both."

They answered with a hailstorm of riflefire, several shots of which exploded through the wall, lifting Chicken into a heap against a chair. In the sudden quiet, you could hear him mumbling, wonder and pride in his eyes. "Goodness, I was right all along," he said, "death does not hurt, not at all." He tried to smile. "There is some genuine comfort in going out this way."

"Darlings," the Kid said, peeking out the window. "I believe they have a cannon."

In horror, we watched them tend to the business of preparing to blast us hellward. My heart was strangely quiet and I had a moment in which I wished for a long life and many healthy heirs. Then, way off, one trooper was waving his arms, and I eased myself into a darker frame of mind.

The first shell split a corner of the building, currency flying up in a tornado of dust and heat.

"Bye-bye." It was Perceval, pointing to his chest. A spear of wood had wedged in his belly. "Let these be my last words: I have seen the good times and the bad; the good are better?"

Twenty minutes later, I was coldcocked. Doc, the Kid and I were in a corner, huddled, occasionally returning fire, but mostly buried in a growing mountain of debris. I shook myself awake twice, I remember, once coming to and finding Doc laughing, saying his was the disposition of a true outlaw—happy and dramatic. The last time I awoke to steady sobbing from the Kid, the Doc cuddling him and murmuring about solace and deserved vistas. Then I was out for good, sinking under a sea of darkness and curiously refreshing dreams—sinking past care and want and stupidity. Even past fear.

That was thirty-one years ago, and I have not been close to death or such fine folks since. I live with the Kid, a virtual female now, whom I call Sweetness or Betty according to my moods. We are aged and surely cut off from a place in the rare airs of paradise, but I have only one regret: that I was not conscious when Doc died.

The Verdigris Kid, my fairy, says there was a lull in the fighting, then the Doc stood, his silk vest somewhat tattered, brushed himself off, grinned. "A man should be gleeful," Doc said, "and do a thing without regard for consequence or ramification." Then, with poise, he walked to his ravaged Dodge, dusted the driver's spot and sat, still and solemn, his scattergun in the cradle of his arms, his expression empty as map space, as if he were gazing, as I now imagine it, into the last chapters of his autobiography—the parts wherein he takes it in the neck. And arm. And old, good heart.

THE FINAL PROOF OF FATE
AND CIRCUMSTANCE

He decided to begin his story with death, saying it was an
uncommonly dark night near El Paso with an uncommon
fog, thick and all the more frightful because it was unexpected, like ice or a Ringling parade of elephants tramping across
the desert from horizon to horizon, each moody and terribly
violent. He was driving on the War Road, two lanes that
came up on the south side of what was then the Proving
Grounds, narrow and without shoulders, barbed-wire fences
alongside, an Emergency Call Box every two miles, on one
side the Franklin Mountains, on the other a boundless insult
of waste; his car, as I now imagine it, must have been a
DeSoto or a Chrysler, heavy with chrome and a grill like a
ten-thousand-pound smile, a car carefully polished to a fierce
shine, free of road dirts and bug filth, its inside a statement
about what a person can do with cheesecloth and patience

and affection. "A kind of palace in there," he'd always say. "Hell, I could live out of the backseat." He was twenty-eight then, he remarked, and he came around that corner, taking that long, stomach-settling dip with authority, driving the next several yards like a man innocent of fret or second thought, gripping that large black steering wheel like a man with resolve and the means to achieve it, like a man intimate with his several selves, scared of little and tolerant of much. I imagine him sitting high, chin upturned, eyes squinty with attentiveness, face alight with a dozen gleams from the dash-board, humming a measure of, say, "Tonight We Love" by Bobby Worth, singing a word of romance now and then, the merry parts of the music as familiar to him as a certain road sign or oncoming dry arroyo.

"I'd just come from Ft. Bliss," he said. "I'd played in a golf tournament that day. Whipped Mister Tommy Bolt, Jr. Old Automatic, that's me. Show up, take home the big one." He was full of a thousand human satisfactions, he said— namely, worth and harmonies and renewals. He could hear his clubs rattling in the trunk; he could hear the wind rushing past, warm and dry, and the tires hissing; and he was think-ing to himself that it was a dandy world to be from, a world of easy rewards and sharp pleasures; a world, from the van-tage point of a victory on the golf course, with heft and sense to it, a world in which a person such as himself—an Army lieutenant such as himself, lean and leaderly—could look forward to the elevated and the utmost, the hindmost for those without muscle or brain enough to spot the gladsome among the smuts; yes, it was an excellent world, sure and large enough for a man with finer features than most, a grown-up man with old but now lost Ft. Worth money behind him, and a daddy with political knowledge, and a momma of substance and high habit, and a youth that had in it such things as regular vacations to Miami Beach, plus a six-week course in the correct carving of fowl and fish, plus a boarding school and even enough tragedy, like a sister drowning and never being recovered, to give a glimpse of, say, woe—which is surely the kind of shape you'd like your own daddy's character to have when he's about to round an insignificant corner in the desert, a Ray Austin lyric on his lips, and kill a man.

It was an accident, of course, the State Police noting it was a combination of bad luck—what with the victim standing so that his taillight was obscured—and the elements (meaning, mostly, the fog, but including as well, Daddy said, time and crossed paths and human error and bad judgment and a certain fundamental untidiness). But then, shaken and offended and partly remorseful, my daddy was angry, his ears still ringing with crash noises and the body's private alarms.

"Goddamn," he said, wrestling open a door of his automobile, its interior dusty and strewn with stuffings from the glove box, a Texaco road map still floating in the air like a kite, a rear floormat folded like a tea towel over the front seat, a thump-thump-thump coming from here and there and there and there. It was light enough for him to see the other vehicle, the quarter moon a dim milky spot, the fog itself swirling and seemingly lit from a thousand directions— half dreamland, half spook-house. "There was a smell, too," he told me, his hands fluttering near his face. A smell like scorched rubber and industrial oils, grease and disturbed earth. His trunk had flown open, his clubs—"Spaldings, Tyler, the finest!"—flung about like pick-up sticks. His thoughts, an instant before airy and affirming, were full of soreness and ache; and, for a moment before he climbed back to the road, he watched one of his wheels spinning, on his face the twitches and lines real sorrow makes, that wheel, though useless, still going round and round, its hubcap scratched and dented.

He was aware, he'd say every time he came to this part, of everything—splintered glass and ordinary night sounds and a stiffness deep in his back and a trouser leg torn at the knee and a fruitlike tenderness to his own cheek pulp. "I felt myself good," he said, showing me again how he'd probed and prodded and squeezed, muttering to himself, "Ribs and necks and hips," that old thighbone-hipbone song the fore- most thing on his mind. His brain was mostly in his ears, and his heart beat like someone was banging at it with a claw hammer, and there was a weakness in the belly, he remem- bered, which in another less stalwart sort might have been called nausea but which in this man, he told himself as he struggled to the roadway, was nothing less than the true discomfort that occurs when Good Feeling is so swiftly over- come by Bad.

At first he couldn't find the body. He walked up and down the road, both sides, yelling and peering into the fog, all the time growing angrier with himself, remembering the sudden appearance of that other automobile stopped more on the road than off, the panic that mashed him in the chest, the thud, the heart-flop. "I found the car about fifty yards away," he said, his voice full of miracle and distance as if every time he told the story—and, in particular, the parts that lead from bad to worse—it was not he who approached the smashed

Chevrolet coupe, but another, an alien, a thing of curiosity and alert eyeballs, somebody naive to the heartbreak humankind could make for itself. The rear of that Chevy, Daddy said, was well and thoroughly crunched, trunk lid twisted, fenders crumpled, its glowing brake light dangling, both doors sprung open as if whatever had been inside had left in a fluster of arm- and legwork. My daddy paced around that automobile many times, looking inside and underneath and on top and nearabout, impatient and anxious, then cold and sweaty both. "I was a mess," he said. "I was thinking about Tommy Bolt and the duty officer at the BOQ and my mother and most every little thing." He was crying, too, he said, not sniveling and whimpering, but important adult tears that he kept wiping away as he widened his circle around the Chevy, snot dribbling down his chin, because he was wholly afraid that, scurrying through the scrub-growth and mesquite and prickly cactus and tanglesome weeds, he was going to find that body, itself crumpled, hurled into some unlikely and unwelcome position—sitting or doing a handstand against a bush—or that he was going to step on it, find himself frozen with dread, his new GI shoes smack in the middle of an ooze that used to be chest or happy man's brain. "I kept telling myself Army things," he said one time. "Buck up. Don't be afraid. Do your duty. I told myself to be calm, methodical. Hope for the best, I said."

And so, of course, when he was hoping so hard his teeth hurt and his neck throbbed and his lungs felt like fire, he found it, bounced against a concrete culvert, legs crossed at the ankle, arms folded at the belt, with neither scratch nor bump nor knot nor runny wound, its face a long, scolding discourse on peace or sleep.

"At first, I didn't think he was dead," Daddy told me. He scrambled to the body, said *get up,* said *are you hurt,* said *can you talk, wake up, mister.* His name was Valentine ("Can you believe that name, Tyler?" Daddy'd say, "Morris E. Valentine!") and my daddy put his mouth next to that man's ear canal and hollered and grabbed a hand—"It wasn't at all cold"—and shook it and gave a female's nasty pinch to Valentine's thigh and listened against the man's nose for breaths or a gurgle and felt the neck for a pulse. Then, Daddy said, there wasn't anything to do next but peek at Mr. Valentine's eyes, which were open in something like surprise or consternation and which were as inert and blank and glassy, my daddy said, as two lumps of coal that had lain for ten million years in darkness. It was then, alone and far from home, that he felt the peacefulness come over him like a shadow on a sunny day—a tranquility, huge and fitting like (he said) the sort you feel at the end of fine drama when, with all the deeds done and the ruin dealt out fairly, you go off to eat and drink some; yup, he said one night, like the end of the War Road itself, a place of dusts and fog and uprooted flora and fuzzy lights where you discover, as the State Police did, a live man and a dead one, the first laughing in a frenzy of horror, the second still and as removed from life as you are from your ancestral fishes, his last thought—evidently a serious one—still plain on his dumb, awful face.

He told me this story again today, the two of us sitting in his backyard, partly in the shade of an upright willow, him in a racy Florida shirt and baggy Bermudas, me in a Slammin' Sammy Snead golf hat and swim trunks. It was hooch, he said, that brought out the raconteur in him, Oso Negro being the fittest of liquors for picking over the past. Lord, he must've gone through a hundred stories this afternoon, all the edge out of his voice, his eyes fixed on the Country Club's fourteenth fairway which runs behind the house. He told one about my mother meeting Fidel Castro. It was a story, he suggested, that featured comedy in large doses and not a little horridness. It had bellow and running hither and hoopla when none was expected. "Far as I could tell," he said, "Fidel was merely a hairy man with a pistol. Plus rabble-rousers." He told another about Panama and the Officers' Club and the Geists, Maizie and Al, and a Memphis industrialist named T. Moncure Yourtees. It was a story that started bad, went some distance in the company of foolishness and youthful hugger-mugger and ended, not with sadness but with mirth. He told about Korea and moosey-maids and sloth and whole families of yellow folk living in squalor and supply problems and peril and cold and, a time later, of having Mister Sam Jones of the Boston Celtics in his platoon. "You haven't known beauty," he said, smiling, "till you see that man dribble. Jesus, it was superior, Tyler."

He told one about some Reservists in Montana or Idaho—one of those barren, ascetic places—and a Training Exercise called Operation Hot Foot which involved, as I recall, scrambling this way and that, eyes peeled for the Red Team, a thousand accountants and farmboys and family men in nighttime camouflage, and a nearsighted Colonel named Krebs who took my daddy bird watching. Daddy said that from his position on a bluff he could see people in green scampering and diving and waving in something approaching terror, but that he and Krebs were looking through binoculars for nest or telltale feather, listening intently for warble or tweet or chirp, the Colonel doing his best, with nose and lipwork, to imitate that genus of fear or hunger or passion a rare flying thing might find appealing. "It was lovely," Daddy said, the two of them putting over two hundred miles on the Jeep in search of Gray's Wing-Notch Swallow or feathered forelimb that had been absent from the planet, Daddy suspected, for an eon. There were trees and buttes and colors from Mister Disney, an austerity, extreme and eternal, that naturally put you in mind of the Higher Plane.

For another hour he went on, his stories addressing what he called the Fine, events in which the hero, using luck and ignorance, managed to avoid the base and its slick companion, the lewd. I heard about a cousin, O. T. Winans, who had it, let it slip away, and snatched it back when least deserved. I learned the two things any dog knows: Can I eat it, or will it eat me? I learned something about people called the Duke and the Earl and the Count and how Tommy Dorsey looked close up. I was touched—not weepy, as my wife Nadine becomes when I tell her a little about my Kappa Alpha days at UTEP or how I stumbled out looking like a dope when I had gone in feeling like a prince. I was in that cozy place few get to these days, that place where your own father—that figure who whomped you and scolded you and who had nothing civil to say about the New York Yankees or General Eisenhower, and who expressed himself at length on the subjects of sideburns and fit reading matter and how a gentleman shines his loafers—yes, that place where your own father admits to being a whole hell of a lot like you, which is sometimes confused and often weak; that place, made habitable by age and self-absorption and fatigue, that says much about those heretofore pantywaist emotions like pity and fear.

Then, about four o'clock, while the two of us stood against his cinderblock fence, watching a fivesome of Country Club ladies drag their carts up the fairway, the sun hot enough to satisfy even William Wordsworth, Daddy announced he had a new story, one which he'd fussed over in his brain a million times but one which, on account of this or that or another thing, he'd never told anyone. Not my momma Elaine. Not my uncle Lyman. Not his sisters, Faith and Caroline. His hand held on my forearm, squeezing hard, and I could see by his eyes, which were watery and inflamed by something I now know as determination, and by his wrinkled, dark forehead and by his knotted neck muscles—by all these things, I knew this story would feature neither the fanciful nor the foreign—neither bird nor military mess-up, nor escapade, nor enterprise in melancholy; it would be, I suspected as he stared at me as though I were no more related to him than that brick or that rabbit-shaped cloud, about mystery, about the strange union of innocence and loss, which sometimes passes for wisdom, and about the downward trend of human desires. There was to be a moral, too; and it was to be, like most morals, obvious and tragic.

This was to be, I should know, another death story, this related to Valentine's the way one flower—a jonquil, for instance—is related to another, like a morning glory, the differences between them apparent, certain and important; and it was to feature a man named X, Daddy said; a man, I realized instantly, who was my father himself, slipped loose of the story now by time and memory and fortunate circumstance. X was married now, I was told, to an upstanding woman and he had equally fine children, among them a youth near my own age, but X had been married before and it would serve no purpose, I was to know, for the current to know about the former, the past being—my daddy said—a thing of regret and diminishment. I understood, I said, understanding further that this woman—my daddy's first wife!— was going to die again as she had died before.

She was a French woman, Daddy said, name of Annette D'Kopman, and X met her in September 1952 at the 4th Army Golf Tournament in San Antonio, their meeting the result of happenstance and X's first-round victory over the professional you now recognize as Mister Orville Moody. "X was thirty-one then," Daddy said, filling his glass with more rum, "the kind of guy who took his celebrating seriously." I listened closely, trying to pick out those notes in his voice you might call mournful or misty. There were none, I'm pleased to say, just a voice heavy with curiosity. "This Annette person was a guest of some fancy-pants," my daddy was saying, and when X saw her, he suspected it was love. I knew that emotion, I thought, it having been produced in me the first time I saw Nadine. I recalled it as a steady knocking in the heartspot, as well as a brain troubled with a dozen thoughts. This Annette, my daddy said, was not particularly gorgeous, but she had, according to X, knuckles that he described as wondrous, plus delicate arches and close pores and deep sockets and a method of getting from oven to freezer with style enough to make you choke or ache in several body parts. So, Daddy said, X and Annette were married the next week, the attraction being mutual, a Mexican JP saying plenty, for twenty dollars, about protection and trust and parting after an extended life of satisfactions, among the latter being health, robust offspring and daily enjoyments.

As he talked, my daddy's face had hope in it, and some pride, as though he were with her again, thirty years from the present moil, squabbling again (as he said), about food with unlikely and unfamiliar vegetables it it, or ways of tending to the demands of the fallen flesh. X and Annette lived at Ft. Sam Houston, he the supply officer for the second detachment, she a gift to dash home to. "It wasn't all happy times," Daddy was saying, there being shares of blue spirits and hurt feelings and misunderstandings as nasty as any X had since had with his present wife. "There was drinking," my daddy said, "and once X smacked her." Still, there was hugging and driving to Corpus Christi and evenings with folks at the Officers' Club and swimming. I imagined them together and—watching him now slumped in his chair, the sun a burning disc over his shoulder—I saw them as an earlier version of Nadine and me: ordinary as dollar bills and doing well to keep a healthful distance from things depraved and hurtful. The lust part, he said, wore off, of course, the thing left behind being close enough to please even the picky and stupid. Then she died.

I remember thinking that this was the hard part, the part wherein X was entitled to go crazy and do a hundred destructive acts, maybe grow miserly and sullen, utter an ugly phrase or two. Certainly drink immoderately. I was wrong, Daddy said. For it was death so unexpected, like one in a fairy tale, that there was only time for the wet howl a dog makes and seventy hours of sweaty, dreamless sleep. "X didn't feel rack or nothing," Daddy said. "Not empty, not needful, nor abused by any dark forces." X was a blank—shock, a physician called it—more rock than mortal beset with any of the mundane hardships. "X did his job," Daddy said, "gave his orders, went and came, went and came." X watched TV, his favorite being Garry Moore's "I've Got a Secret," read a little in the lives of others, ate at normal hours, looked as determined as your typical citizen, one in whom there was now a scorched, tender spot commonly associated with sentiment and hope. Colonel Buck Wade concluded the funeral arrangements—civilian, of course—talking patiently with X, offering a shoulder and experience and pith. "X kept wondering when he'd grieve," Daddy said. Everyone looked for the signs: outburst of the shameful sort, tactless remark, weariness in the eyes and carriage. But there was only numbness, as if X were no more sentient than a clock or Annette herself.

"Now comes the sad part," my daddy said, which was not the ceremony, X having been an Episcopalian, or the burial because X never got that far. Oh, there was a service, X in his pressed blues, brass catching the light like sparkles, the minister, a Dr. Hammond Ellis, trying through the drift and bent of learnedness itself to put the finest face on a vulgar event, reading one phrase about deeds and forgiveness and another about the afterworld and its steady tempers, each statement swollen with a succor or a joy, words so impossible with knowledge and acceptance that X sat rigid, his back braced against a pew, his pals unable to see anything in his eyes except emptiness. No, the sadness didn't come then—not with prayer, not with the sniffling of someone to X's left, not at the sight of the casket itself toted outside. The sadness came, my daddy said, in the company of the driver of the family car in which X rode alone. "The driver was a kid," Daddy told me, "twenty, maybe younger, name of Monroe." Whose face, I learned, had through it a thousand conflicting thoughts—of delight and of money and of nooky and of swelter like today's. Monroe, I was to know, was the squatty sort, the kind who's always touchy about his height, with eyeballs that didn't say anything about his inner life, and chewed nails and a thin tie and the wrong brown shoes for a business otherwise associated with black, plus an ugly spot on his neck that could have been a pimple or ingrown hair. "Stop," X said, and Monroe stared at him in the mirror. "What—?" Monroe was startled. "I said stop." They were halfway to the gravesite, funeral coach in front, a line of cars with lights on in back. "Stop here. Do it now." X was pointing to a row of storefronts on Picacho Street—laundry, a barber's, a Zale's jewelry.

My daddy said he didn't know why Monroe so quickly obeyed X, but I realize now that Monroe was just responding to that tone in my father's voice that tells you to leave off what you're doing—be it playing canasta, eating Oreos with your mouth open or mumbling in the crisis moments of "Gunsmoke"—and take up politeness and order and respectfulness. It's a note that encourages you toward the best, the most responsible in yourself, and it has in it a hint of the nasty consequences that await if you do not. So the Cadillac pulled over, Monroe babbling "uh-uh-uh," and X jumped out, saying, "Thank you, Monroe, you may go on now."

It was here that I got stuck trying to explain it to Nadine, trying to show that funeral coach already up the street, Monroe having a difficult time getting his car in gear while behind him, stopped, a line of headlamps stretching well back, a few doors opening, the folks nearest startled and wild-eyed and looking to each other for help, and X, his hat set aright, already beginning a march down the sidewalk, heels clicking, shoulders squared, a figure of precision and care and true strength. I told Nadine, as my daddy told me, about the cars creeping past, someone calling out, Colonel Buck Wade stopping and ordering, then shouting for X to get in. X didn't hear, Daddy said. Wade was laughable, his mouth working in panic, an arm waving, his own wife tugging at his sleeve, himself almost as improbable as that peculiar bird my daddy and another colonel had spent a day hunting years ago.

"X didn't know where he was going," Daddy said. To be true, he was feeling the sunlight and the heavy air and hearing, as if with another's ears, honks and shouts, but X said he felt moved and, yes, driven, being drawn away from something, not forward to another. The sadness lay on him then, my daddy said; and this afternoon, I saw it again in his face, a condition as permanent as the shape of your lips or your natural tendency to be silly. X went into an ice-cream parlor, and here I see him facing a glass-fronted counter of Tutti-Frutti and Chocolate and Pineapple Sherbet, and behind it a teenage girl with no more on her mind than how to serve this one, then another and another until she could go home. X ordered Vanilla, Daddy said, eating by the spoonful, deliberately and abstractedly, as if the rest of his life—a long thing he felt he deserved—depended on this moment. It was the best ice-cream X ever ate, Daddy said, and for three cones he thought of nothing, not bleakness, not happiness, not shape, not beauty, not thwarts, not common distress—not anything the bootless brain turns toward out of tribulation.

It was then, my daddy said, that X realized something— about the counter-girl, the ice-cream itself, Colonel Buck

Wade, even the children and the new wife he would have one day, and the hundreds of years still to pass—and this insight came to X with such force and speed that he felt light-headed and partially blind, the walls tipping and closing in on him, the floor rising and spinning, a mountain of sundae crashing over his shoulders and neck; he was going to pass out, X knew, and he wondered what others might say, knowing that his final thought—like Mr. Valentine's in one story—was long and complex and featured, among its parts, a scene of hope followed by another of misfortune and doom.

When Nadine asked me an hour ago what the moral was, I said, "Everything is fragile." We were in the kitchen, drinking Buckhorn, she in her pj's; and I tried, though some overthrown by drink and a little breathless, to explain, setting the scene and rambling, mentioning ancient times and sorrow and pride in another. It was bad. I put everything in—the manner of sitting, how the air smelled when Daddy went inside, gesture that had significance, what my own flesh was doing. But I was wrong. Completely wrong. For I left out the part where I, sunburned but shivering, wandered through X's house, one instant feeling weepy, another feeling foolish and much aged.

The part I left out shows me going into his kitchen, reading the note my momma wrote when she went to Dallas to visit my aunt Dolly; and it shows me standing in every room, alien in that place as a sneak-thief, handling their bric-a-brac and Daddy's tarnished golf trophies, sitting on the edge of the sofa or the green, shiny lounger, in the guest bathroom opening the medicine cabinet, curiosity in me as strong as the lesser states of mind. It's the episode that has all the truth in it—and what I'll tell Nadine in the morning. I'll describe how I finally entered Daddy's room and stood over his bed, listening to him snore, the covers clenched at his chest, saying to myself, as he did long ago, headbone and chinbone, legbone and armbone. Yes, when I tell it, I'll put in the part wherein a fellow such as me invites a fellow such as him out to do a thing—I'm not sure what—that involves effort and sacrifice and leads, in an hour or a day, to that throb and swell fellows such as you call triumph.